Newton's Mill

The Town That Almost Forgot Christmas

By Ray Newman and Bob Willey

Ray Newman (signature)

Text copyright ©2006 Ray Newman and Bob Willey

PROLOGUE

The town of Newton's Mill has a problem. It's a problem that threatens to tear the town apart and destroy one of its happiest times. It's a problem faced by many cities and towns today. What is the problem? Well, before I tell you what it is let me tell you a little bit about Newton's Mill.

The town began when Colonel Rufus Newton, returning from the Civil War, decided to build a mill to give the local farmers a place to bring their grain and other crops for grinding and shipment to the rest of the country. Now the land around the mill was fertile and the farmers were many so it wasn't long before it prospered and the town grew. For more than a hundred years Newton's Mill brought people from much of the country to work there and to establish the stores, services and homes of a thriving community.

The main street through town was named, appropriately, Main Street, and it was part of the interstate that ran through Newton's Mill from the big city to the East. It was down this street that the people came that put an end to the mill. When the folks from that big city to the East discovered Newton's Mill, and the cheap land around it, they began to grow a new crop in the fields.

Houses.

The local farmers, offered enormous sums for their property, sold out and moved further west and settled in condos and homes near the ocean. Which left Newton's Mill with little else to do but shut down. Of course, by that time the new homes and increased population had given rise to other business and industries to keep the town going.

And one of the biggest businesses in the town was the department store owned by J. B. Nickels. And, quite a place it was. Nickels sold everything from soup to nuts, literally. The center of the store featured what was called a "Food Court" where you could buy everything from soup to nuts. But the store also featured appliances, entertainment equipment, clothing and a hundred other items to take the money of those well-to-do newcomers from the big city to the East. Nickels was a master at marketing and was always at the forefront of every new fad or development that would make a profit.

That's why Santa appeared in the Nickels' Department Store and Shopping Mall, long before that holiday.

Which brings us to the problem.

Christmas.

Now you would think that Christmas would be the one holiday that everyone could agree on. But you would be wrong. And the whole centerpiece of the problem was the annual Nativity Scene that Colonel Newton first put up the year after he opened the mill. Then it sat in front of the mill and had been carved from wood, life size, by a local artisan, aptly named Floyd Carver. It was after the mill closed that the Nativity Scene was moved to the lawn in front of the Court House, which also served as the seat of local government, and thus created the problem. It seems that some of the folks that decided to make Newton's Mill their home didn't take too kindly to the set being on "government property". Didn't seem to make any difference to them that, until they took exception to it, it had sat there every Christmas for a lot of years without causing anyone to complain.

Tuesday

So it was that this year the City Council decided to take up the problem. They called an open session for the regularly scheduled Tuesday night meeting. Meetings were held on Tuesday's so as not to interfere with three-day holidays that included a Monday; Wednesday night choir practice at the local churches and Friday night football . Thursday's just never seemed to catch on, although they tried a couple of Thursdays several years ago. Anyway, the courthouse was packed to overflowing that Tuesday night and a lot of the long time residents of Newton's Mill were on hand to watch the show.

And quite a show it was going to be.

There were representatives from the AAA. No, not the Auto Club. They were from the Atheists and Agnostics Association. Seems they were convinced that celebrating Christmas was a waste of time considering there really wasn't a God and it was a waste of the taxpayer's money as well. I think they sort of threw that last part in.

And then there was the local women's auxiliary of W.H.E.N. or **W**omen **H**oping For **E**quality **N**ow. They weren't against the display, just wanted to alternate a boy baby and a girl baby in the manger. Sort of a politically correct Christ child.

And then there was Rufus J. Pettifogger. He was in attendance representing the OARD, the Organization Against Religious Displays. Which, as we all know, will represent just about anybody. Rufus is, well, let's just say that Rufus handles the smaller cases. But this could be his big chance. At least he hopes so.

Of course we can't forget the members of the Newton's Mill Pastoral Association. They are represented by Pastor Roger Rogers of the Methodist Episcopal Church. Those two churches merged a few years back over some sort of doctrinal disagreement. He is joined by Monsignor O'Rourke of the Catholic Diocese and the Right Reverend Artemis Brown of Bethlehem Baptist Church. Seems they can all agree on something now and then.

Oh, and over there in the far corner of the room is the Enlightened One, Swami Mohammed Abdullah Jones. Nobody knows why he's here. Come to think of it, he doesn't even know where here is since most of his enlightenment comes from controlled substances.

Nearly the whole town has turned out for this meeting. The seats are full and folks are standing up along the walls, across the back and even outside in the hallway where they can barely hear but wouldn't want to miss anything. Looks like the Mayor and the City Council have their work cut out for them tonight.

****

"This meeting will come to order!"

That's Mayor G.D. Steward. He's lived in this town his whole life. His Grandpa worked in the Mill before it closed, come to think of it, so did his Dad and both his Uncles. In those days most near everybody worked there. He was first elected Mayor six years ago and is in the middle of his second term. Depending on how this whole thing turns out it could be his last.

Banging his gavel on the desk he shouted above the noise of the crowd. "I said, this meeting will come to order." Standing behind the desk and waiting for the talking to subside, he was thinking, *"Look at all these people. First time I've ever seen more than one or two at these meetings. This might be a bigger issue than I thought."*

Finally the room had quieted enough for him to speak without shouting. "Glad to see so many public spirited folks in attendance tonight. And I'm sure we all know why we're here." They sure did. The local paper had been running front-page stories on it, and it was the talk of everyone in the community.

"But, just for those of you who might still wonder, we're gathered here tonight to decide whether our annual Nativity Scene should remain in it's historical place in front of the Courthouse, or not.

I suppose there are some here who would like to speak to the subject so we will begin by opening the meeting for discussion."

"Mayor Steward." That was Ira Freethinker of the Atheists and Agnostics group. His real name was John Smart but he thought Freethinker was a bit more impressive. "As a representative of the Atheists and Agnostics Association I must register our disapproval of the

public display of this obviously fictional historical occurrence."

"Amen." That was from Freethinker's right hand man, Phil Faithless, not his real name either.

"What!" Freethinker jerked his head toward Phil.

"Sorry, I mean, right on."

"That's better." Freethinker continued. "This is definitely a furtherance of one religion over another as well as a blatant waste of the taxpayer's money. It would be better displayed in the front window of J.B. Nickels store." And with that he sat down.

"Thank you for your input, Mr. Freethinker." Mayor Steward tried to be as fair and impartial as he could be but it was hard to keep the smile off his face. "Is there anyone else who would like to speak to this matter?"   "Yes, Mayor Steward, I would like to address the council, please." That was Eloise

Simonet, president of W.H.E.N. She was a large lady in size but rather narrow in perspective.

"Ms. Simonet, you have the floor."

"Thank you, Mr. Mayor. As everyone knows there is a great deal of discrimination against the women of our modern society and this Nativity scene is just another example of that situation. While we do not object, per se, to the display of this cultural icon we do feel that there should be some accommodation to those of us who feel disenfranchised by society in general and discriminated in particular by this display." She could go on like this all night, and would have if the Mayor had not jumped in when she paused for a breath.

"Ms. Simonet, get to the point please."

"Well," Eloise drew herself up to her full five foot three inch height and looked at the Mayor over the tops of her glasses. "It seems only equitable that the small image of the child in the manger, obviously a boy child, should be replaced on alternate days with a child of the opposite sex."

"Excuse me?" The Mayor could hardly believe what he was hearing. "You want to alternate a boy and girl child in the manger as a form of political correctness?"

"Exactly, Mr. Mayor. For too long the women of this society have..." The rest of her statement was drowned out by the laughter and derision of most of the people in the room. Even Ira Freethinker thought it was funny. And he hardly ever laughed at anything. Ms. Simonet turned a rather unbecoming shade of purple and returned to her seat.

"Thank you for that interesting input." Mayor Steward said when the laughter had died down.

"Now, if there are no other..."

"Excuse me, Mr. Mayor." It was Rufus Pettifogger. "I represent the OARD in this area and would like to speak on this matter."

"Of course you would," thought the Mayor. "Please make your statement." He said as he waved Rufus forward.

"Thank you," Rufus said, as he stepped to the front of the room. "We of the Organization Against Religious Displays would like to go on record as being adamantly opposed to this, what do you call it, this Nativity Scene being placed on government property. This is obviously a case of local government aligning itself with religion and is a clear violation of the separation of Church and State as outlined in the Constitution. After all, Christmas is simply a national holiday celebrating something that is nothing more than an ethnic folk festival."

"Just a minute, you pompous windbag!"

Oh my, that was the Right Reverend Artemis "Bruiser" Brown, and he was not going to let that statement go unchallenged.

"By what perverted right of legalese misdirection could you possibly justify calling the birth of our Lord and Savior an ethnic folk festival?"

"Order here, order." Mayor Steward could see that this might get seriously out of hand if he didn't do something quick. Reverend Brown had been a ferocious linebacker and a terror of opposition backfields before he gave up the mayhem for the cross. And he had been known to deliver a powerful sermon with either hand.

"Reverend Brown, please control yourself." The Mayor said, as he banged his gavel once more. Rufus Pettifogger, feeling that discretion was the better part of valor had quickly made his way back to his seat as the Mayor tried to calm the situation.

"I'm sorry, Mr. Mayor." The Reverend respected Mayor Steward for his fairness and spoke more softly. "It's just that what I see happening here is an outrage. Removing Christ from Christmas is an abomination before the Lord." This last was met by cries of "Here, Here and Amen." from various parts of the room. "This threatens the very heart of Christianity and I and my fellow men of God cannot stand idly by and watch the degradation of this holy event."

"Alright, Reverend Brown. You're objections are duly noted. Are there any others who would like to speak to the issue?" Mayor Steward looked around the room and seeing no other hands raised banged his gavel on the desk.

"Alright then, open discussions are closed. We will now poll the members of the Council for their votes on the matter at hand. "Given the emotions surrounding this issue," Mayor Steward had stood up and was looking at the council members seated to his right and to his left. "I feel that each council member should weigh his vote carefully. Does anyone of the council members wish to be the first to cast his vote?"

The members squirmed a little in their seats as a hush fell over the room. The political futures of each member could very well rise or fall with their stand on the issue.

"Well." The Mayor asked.

Still no one seemed eager to go first. Finally the Mayor made the decision for them.

"Councilman Archibald, you are the senior member of the council, having served the longest of all of us. So, out of respect for your many years of service why don't you be the first to cast your vote?"

There were several groans from those gathered in the hall. "We'll be here all night. He's the biggest windbag in the town," whispered someone in the back row, to nods of assent from those within earshot.

After a long pause Councilman Archibald stood slowly. Looking around the room he cleared his throat and began to speak in his most officious voice. "Thank you Mr. Mayor, for your acknowledgment of my many long years of faithful service to this fine community."

"Here he goes." the Mayor thought.   "Speaking on behalf of my loyal constituents, who have seen fit to elect me to this chair over these past years, I feel an obligation to discharge my duties as

befits someone who has the utmost appreciation of this grand and glorious governmental system."

"Get on with it, Archie." The Mayor whispered. "Elections aren't until next year."

"Uh, right you are, Mr. Mayor." Councilman Archibald stood quietly for a moment, unusual for him, and looked around the room. "I see many faces here that I have known since we were children growing up together here in the fine community of Newton's Mill. Faces of people who have depended on my wisdom and judgment to make the right decisions regarding our fair community."

"Archie!" The Mayor spoke louder this time. "How do you vote?"

"Oh, yes, of course, the vote. Well, Mr. Mayor and concerned citizens of this community, I, Councilman Nathaniel Archibald vote..." He paused for just a second as everyone in the audience leaned forward in anticipation. "...in favor of the traditional celebration that has been the cornerstone of our worship since this fair city grew out of the dust of the plains..."

Mayor Steward banged his gavel, cutting him off in mid sentence. "Let the record show that Archie votes yes."

Councilman Archibald sat quickly, with the look of a man just deprived of oxygen.

Turning to the man to his left Mayor Steward spoke. "J.B., you're next. How do you vote?"

J.B. was none other than J.B. Nickels, owner of the biggest store in town where they sold everything from soup to nuts. Oh, but you know that already. He owed his seat at the council table to a dynamic and expensive campaign. He outspent all his rivals ten times over. But, he could afford it. This should be interesting.

"Mr. Mayor," J.B. also stood as he spoke. "Unlike my esteemed and long winded colleague I see absolutely, I say, I see no, reason for the use of public funds to benefit one small segment of this community."

There were some comments from the crowd over that statement and the Right Reverend Brown looked like he was about to erupt again.

"Since man first evolved into a thinking being," J. B. continued on without a pause. "His thoughts have always been on the important things in life. Money! And the more money he makes the more he has to spend in the stores of our community."

"You mean like in your store, right J.B." a voice called from the crowd.

"Right, er, I mean, well, yes in my store, and others."

"J.B. this wouldn't have anything to do with the fact that last year we decided not to buy a new Nativity Scene from you would it?" The Mayor asked.

"Well, now that you mention it Mr. Mayor I think you will remember that I offered the new set to the city for just 10% over my cost."

"How much, J.B.?"

"Uh, well, 20% over my..."

"What?"   "It was a good deal, anyway."

"Come on, J.B. how do you vote?"

"I vote...no!"

"Let the record show that J.B. votes no. Now, it's your turn Councilman Humble."

Councilman Hebert Humble sat next to J.B. and was one of the gentlest men in the town of Newton's Mill. His wife, Bertha, however, was not. And much to Councilman Humble's dismay she always sat in the front row directly in front of his seat at the council table. To say that she often influenced his vote with a word or a look would be an understatement.

"Well," he spoke softly, hardly looking up. "It is sort of a nice tradition..."

"Hebert!" His wife whispered in a voice loud enough to be

heard in

the corridor outside the room.

"...but, of course, on the other hand..."

"If you vote no you lose my vote in the next election." A voice called from the crowd. "Mine, too." Echoed another followed by several comments in the same vein.

"...but then Christmas has always given me a warm feeling..."

"Hebert!!!" His wife again.

"...of course, it could have been indigestion..."

"Hebert, quit hemming and hawing and vote." The Mayor looked down the table at him.

"...alright...I vote in favor of..."   "Hebert!!!" This time Mrs. Humble nearly jumped to her feet.

"...voting no!"

With this last Councilman Humble collapsed back into his seat. Once again his dear wife had humiliated him in public. *"Oh well,"* He thought. *"I suppose I should be used to it by now."*

"Let the record show that Councilman Humble voted no, finally." Mayor Steward spoke to the secretary who sat at a small table just to the side of the Council table. "You're next, Mrs. Johnson."

The fourth member of the Council was Mary Beth Johnson. Other than the Mayor she was probably the best-informed member of the Council. She had been the Valedictorian of her Newton High graduating class and had involved herself in community work for many years. She was also the editor of the Newton Mill Press and one of the Mayor's strongest supporters.

"Mr. Mayor," Mary Beth stood and looked around the room as she spoke. "I really don't understand why this has become an issue. We support the 4th of July with fireworks paid for by the city. We support Halloween with a big party for the kids at the National Guard Armory, paid for by the city. And, on Thanksgiving we have baskets for the needy, also paid for by the city. So, I see nothing wrong with using city funds, or city property for the display of the Nativity Scene. After all, it sets a mood of good will and peace for the community. Therefore I say yes to the placement of the scene in front of this very courthouse, where it has been every Christmas since the Mill closed." "Thank you, Mary Beth. Let the record show that Councilwoman Johnson votes yes."

"Mr. Mayor." The Secretary spoke for the first time that evening. "We have two votes in favor and two votes opposed."

"Ahem," Councilman Archibald cleared his throat as he rose to his feet. "The Charter of this fair city specifically states that in the event of a tie among the Council members the issue is to be decided solely by the vote of the Mayor, who is the elected representative of this community."

"I know that, Archie." The Mayor said. "I know that."

"In other words, Mr. Mayor, it's up to you." Someone called from the crowd.

"That's right, how do you vote," called another. Then there were several other voices raised with the same question.

"I was afraid of this." The Mayor thought. *"I'm not ready to be the deciding vote on this because I'm not even sure how I feel about it."*

"Ahem!" Councilman Archibald cleared his throat once again. "Yes, Mr. Mayor. It is up to you. How do you vote?"

The crowd erupted into shouting as each faction tried to influence the Mayor's vote in their favor.

"ORDER! ORDER!" The Mayor continued to bang his gavel on the table until the room quieted. "According to the city charter I have until the next meeting to render my decision. Since that meeting will be held next Tuesday I will wait until then to cast my vote. Let the record show that there is no further business." He banged the gavel once more. "This meeting is adjourned." He then left the Council chambers quickly as the uproar began again.

****

"How did the Council meeting go, G.D.?" The Mayor's wife, Helen, had called him G.D. ever since they first met as freshmen at Newton High. He was a skinny kid with glasses and she was the most beautiful girl he had ever seen. Of course, in a town as small as Newton's Mill was in those days that's probably because he hadn't seen that many girls, pretty or not. But they hit it off from the first day and it was no surprise to anyone that they would get married sooner or later. Which they did, sooner than later. And now it had been fifteen years, a boy just turning twelve and a girl who died just after her first birthday. And except for that it had been a pretty great fifteen years.

"Did you get the problem of the Nativity Scene settled?"

"No, not just yet."

"What's that mean?"

"It means that we had a lot of input, lots of emotion and concern and." The Mayor paused.

"And?" Helen asked.

"And a tie vote."

"A tie? I don't believe it. You mean there were actually council members who voted against the Nativity Scene. Why, that's like voting against Christmas." Helen poured G.D. a cup of coffee as he sat down at the kitchen table. "Tell me about ...wait a minute. You said it was a tie vote?"

"That's right, two for, two against."

"Then that means you have the deciding vote."

"Exactly."

"So, did you break the tie and vote for the Nativity Scene?"

G.D. sat quietly, stirring his coffee, not really wanting to answer.

"G.D. You did vote for it, didn't you?"

"Well, not exactly."

"Not exactly? What does that mean?"

"Well, I postponed my decision until the meeting next week."

"I don't understand. You are for the display, aren't you?" Helen looked closely at her husband. She knew him like a book and seemed to sense his indecision. "I mean, after all, it's a tradition here in Newton's Mill. That set has been a centerpiece of our Christmas season for, what, more than a hundred years?"

"I know, Helen. But, well, Newton's Mill isn't the town it used to be."

"You can say that again. But what has that got to do with this?"

"I guess, what I'm saying is, I have to be a representative of all the people of this town. Not just those we have grown up with our whole lives. My vote needs to reflect the will of the people of the town. All the people." "So, what are you going to do?" Helen poured herself a cup of coffee and sat at the table across from him.

"I don't know. I suppose I'll spend the next week talking to folks in town, get their perspective on it. See what the consensus of opinion is. You know me well enough to know that I won't make a decision without weighing everything."

She knew. "I understand. I guess when you put it that way you really do need to make a decision that reflects the majority. But, somehow, I'm afraid that this is just the beginning of the end of our traditions."

"I know. That scares me, too. Traditions are a big part of who we are. What this town is. I'm not sure I like what we're becoming."

"So, tell me about the meeting." Helen could see that this was beginning to get to G.D. and so she tried to change the subject.

"Ah, the meeting." He smiled for the first time since coming home. "You would have loved it."

"Really"

"Yes, we had people there from just about every point of view imaginable. And some of their points of view were a little unimaginable."

"Like what." Helen smiled. She could see the change of focus was going to work.

"We had a group from the AAA."

"The auto club? What do they care about this matter?"

"No, not the auto club. The Atheist and Agnostics Association. They, of course, were opposed to the display of this obviously fictional historical occurrence."

"Fictional historical occurrence?"

"Their words, not mine. They suggested that we display it in the front window at J.B.'s store."

"Oh, I'm sure J.B. loved that."

"Then we heard from the ever lovely Eloise Simonet,"

"Oh no. The lady from W.H.E.N.? What did she have to say?"

"She wanted equal representation in the manger."

"What?"

"Equal representation in the manger. One day a boy baby, the next a girl baby. You know a coed Nativity, so to speak."

Helen was laughing so hard there were tears in her eyes. "You can't be serious."

"Well, she sure was. However, the crowd sort of shut her down on that one."

"I'll bet. I'm almost afraid to ask who else spoke."

"Well, just who do you suppose would have an interest in this particular situation?"

Helen looked closely at G.D. "Who else?"

"Come on. I'm sure you can figure it out." G.D. was starting to have fun with this now.

"Oh wait. I know. I know. The OARD!" Helen almost shouted.

"Right you are. Our very own Rufus Pettifogger. He said Christmas was nothing more than an ethnic folk festival."

"An ethnic what?"

"An ethnic folk festival."

"How did that fly with the crowd?"

"Reverend Brown almost blitzed him."

"I don't blame him."

"Finally got everyone quieted down and asked for a vote."

"Who was first?"

"Actually no one wanted to go first. So I called on Archie."

"Oh, really. And you got home this early."

"Now, Helen, he doesn't really talk that much."

"Excuse me?"

"Well, okay, he does. Anyway, after his usual stump speech I had to remind him that elections weren't until next year and got him to vote."

"And he voted...?"

"In favor of the display.

"Good. Who was next?"

"J.B."

"Don't tell me. He voted no."

"Yep."

"Still upset because we didn't buy that Nativity Scene from him last year?"   "Uh huh. Then Hebert's turn came."

"Was Bertha in the front row?"

"Her usual seat."

"So?"

"Took him a while but he voted no, just the way Bertha wanted him to."

"Why would she be against it?"

"Just been nominated for the Presidency of the local W.H.E.N. Chapter."

"That would do it."

"Mary Beth was last and she voted in favor of the display."

"Good for her."

"But that resulted in a tie vote and of course Archie was quick to point out that it was my responsibility to cast the deciding vote."

"I'm not surprised."

"So, I continued the vote to next week, adjourned the meeting and beat a hasty retreat out the back door before anybody could question me."

"That's my G.D. Bravery in the face of overwhelming odds." Helen giggled.

"Very funny. Let's go to bed. It's been a long day."

****

Wednesday

So, it would seem the pressure is on the Mayor. But, if you

want to see real pressure let's look in on J.B. Nickels getting his new crop of Santas all fired up for the Christmas Season, or as J.B. says, "Christmas just comes once a year, so we gotta move lots of stuff out of here."

Right now he is standing in front of a row of some of the sorriest looking Santas to ever be assembled. Since J.B. always has several Santas placed strategically around his store he needs more than just one or two. But this crop was the worst he had seen in many years. Of the dozen candidates standing in a ragged line in front of him there wasn't a natural looking Santa in the bunch. They were either too tall, too short, too skinny or, believe it or not, too fat. *"What a disgraceful looking bunch,"* J.B. thought.

Turning to one of his assistants he whispered, "Is this the best you can do? Where did you get this crop of losers? From the homeless shelter?" J.B. was never one to care much about what he said. He always figured his money gave him the right to be nasty. And he always took advantage of that right.

"Well, Sir," the assistant answered, "The pay for this job is so low nobody wants to do it. The homeless shelter was the only place I could get anyone to even try for the job."

"Too low?" J.B. snarled. "What kind of money do they expect just for sitting around on their bottoms and listening to greedy little kids tell them what they want for Christmas?"

"Right, Sir." The assistant agreed. It wasn't a good idea to argue with J.B. if you wanted to keep working for him.

"Alright, let's get on with it." J. B. walked to the first Santa in line. He was a skinny fellow, with a scraggly beard and glasses. *"Definitely not the Santa type."* thought J.B. "Let me hear you say Ho-Ho-Ho."

"Ho-Ho-Ho," squeaked the candidate. Too scared to even look at J.B.

"Is that your idea of what a Santa Ho-ho-ho would sound like? That is pitiful. Get out of here."

J.B. moved on to the second man as the skinny fellow headed for the door as fast as his feet would carry him.

The second man in line was absolutely the fattest man J.B. had ever seen. "How much do you weight?" he asked.

"Around 325 pounds." The man replied.

"A "round" 325 pounds is right. See that Santa chair over there?"

"Yes, sir."

"Go sit in it." The fat man walked, actually waddled, over and sat down heavily in the chair. His stomach hung over his knees as he sat.

J.B. followed him over and watched as he sat down. "Finster," he called to one of his assistants.

"Yes, J.B."

"Come over here and sit down on fatso's lap. If you can."

The assistant tried to sit on the fat man's lap, but there was nothing to sit on. He kept slipping off.

"That's what I thought. You're so fat there won't be anyplace for any of those greedy little brats to sit. Get outta here. I don't need a Santa that fat." He shouted as he pointed toward the door.

"And you really expect me to believe that this guy came from the homeless shelter?" He asked the assistant in charge of recruitment. "They sure must be eating good there."

"Uh, well, no sir. I didn't get him from the homeless shelter. He's my Brother-in-Law and..."

"Your Brother-in-Law?" J.B. shouted. "How many times have I told you no family or friends working here? You might be tempted to give them special privileges."

"I'm sorry, J.B." the assistant stammered.

"You're also fired!" J.B. was never one to mince words. "Finster, you've just been promoted. See if you can't do a better job than Smithers."   "Right J.B." Finster answered.

Moving back to the line of Santas J.B. faced the next man in line. He was at least six inches taller than J.B., clean-shaven and had a glint in his bright blue eyes. J.B. didn't like him, immediately. "How tall are you?" He asked.

"I'm six foot nine, barefooted." The man smiled. J.B. didn't intimidate him at all.

"Barefooted? Well, we don't have much use for barefooted Santas." J.B. snorted.

"Then I'm six foot ten in Santa boots." The tall man was enjoying this. He had met guys like J.B. before.

J.B. stood quietly for a minute. *"This guy isn't afraid of me at all,"* he thought. *"I don't need somebody working for me who isn't afraid of me."*

"Well," he said, as he moved on to the next candidate. "You're too tall. Can't use you."

"J.B. you're just a big windbag." The tall man started laughing as he walked toward the door. "I wouldn't work for you on a bet."

J.B. just ignored him as he faced the next man in line. He always avoided dealing with people he couldn't intimidate. But the tall man's attitude had unnerved him so he finished with the other Santas as quickly as he could. He chose six out of the dozen candidates and sent them off to get fitted for their Santa costumes and begin the second phase of the J.B. Nickels Santa Academy.

****

Now there are some who will tell you that compared to The J.B. Nickels' Santa Academy, Marine Corps Boot Camp is a picnic. J.B. always ran the Academy himself because he didn't trust any of his flunkies to be tough enough. One thing J.B. always counted on was his ability to intimidate anybody. Except, maybe, the big fellow who laughed at him, and Cora his wife. So it was with great anticipation that he faced the six Santas that he had selected.

"Look at you!" He growled as he stepped in front of the first man. "You look like an unmade bed. Pull up those pants. Pull down that shirt."

"Yes J.B."

"And you, how much padding have you got in that suit?" J.B. moved to the next man in line.

"A couple of pillows, Mr. Nickels, sir." The man stammered.

"Well, it ain't enough. Finster." J.B. turned to his assistant. "See that this guy gets more padding."

"Right, J. B." Finster scribbled a note on his pad of paper. "I'll take care of it as soon as we're done here."

"See that you do."

J.B. turned to the next Santa in line and fixed him with a hard stare. "Is that the best you can do with those whiskers?"

"Yes, sir...ugh, I mean no sir..." the poor fellow was petrified.

"Well, what is it? Yes or no?"

"Uh, I guess it's..."

"Oh, never mind. Just get somebody to do something with them so you don't look like you're trying to swallow a porcupine." J. B. started to smile but caught himself just in time. *"Swallowed a porcupine?"* he thought. *"I'll have to remember that. That's funny."*

The last man of the four really stood out from the rest. His Santa suit fit him reasonably well, his beard was presentable and he even had the right amount of padding. J.B. was speechless, almost.

"So, what are trying to do, impress me?" J.B. asked. "Won't get you any more money."

"Yes, J.B." the man answered.

J.B. made his way back to a spot a few feet in front of the four and looked down the line.

"Alright, you six, this is it. Your first day at the J.B. Nickels Santa Academy. Have you all received the 73 page instruction manual?"

"Yes, sir." The six answered, almost in unison.

"Good, then if you will turn to page 22, section 9, paragraph 2 we will get on with it." J. B. pointed to several chairs along the wall. "Take your seats over there."

J.B. began to pace back and forth in front of the Santas. "You there," he said as he pointed to the first of the six. "What does that section say?" "Any child," the man began reading. "Requesting a toy, or toys, not carried or currently out of stock at J.B. Nickels, Inc. shall quickly and effectively be directed to such toy, or toys, mandated by the management and stocked and readily available."

"Very Good." J.B. said as he turned to the next man. "What does the rest of that section say?"

"It says failure to do so will result in immediate dismissal." The second man read.

"Right. And don't any of you forget it."

"Yes J.B." They answered.

"Alright, let's try a little dry run here. You," J.B. pointed to the third man in the line. "What's your name?"

"McGillicudy."

"McGillicudy?"

"Yes sir, Seamus McGillicudy."

"Well, for now we'll just call you Santa McGillicudy. Get over there on that Santa chair. And Finster, you be the five year old kid that wants a red flyer wagon with white sidewall tires."

"Right, J.B." Finster walked over and sat down on McGillicudy's lap and began to suck his thumb.

"Finster, get that thumb out of your mouth. Your not really five years old."

"Sorry, J.B. just trying to get in character."

"Forget character. I don't have all day. Now, McGillicudy, your job is to convince this greedy little kid that he doesn't really want a red flyer wagon with white sidewalls."

"He doesn't?"

"No, what he really wants is a space alien doll."

"A what?" Finster asked.

"A space alien doll. We got stuck with a carload of those little stinkers when that movie left town and we gotta get rid of them." J.B. Snarled. "Okay, let's get started."

"Ho, ho, ho..." McGillicudy laughed. "Have you been a good little boy?"

"McGillicudy! We don't care if the kid has been good or bad, just get down to the basics."

"Right, J.B. So, what do you want for Christmas, little boy?"

"What I really, really, really..."

"FINSTER! Will you just get on with it?"

"A red flyer wagon with white sidewalls." Finster blurted out.

"Ho, ho, ho," McGillicudy chuckled. "We don't have any of those but how about a nice space alien doll?"

"Hold it! Hold it!" J.B. was furious. "Didn't you read page 37, Section 1, Paragraph 8?"

"Not yet." McGillicudy answered.

"Well, for your information it says 'Never admit you do not have a toy or product in stock.' Is that clear?"   "I think so, J.B."

"Get out of there." J.B. grabbed McGillicudy by the shoulder and yanked him out of the chair. "I'll show you how to handle this. Sit on my lap, Finster."

"Yes J.B." Finster sat down slowly.

"Now, little boy, what big expensive toy do you want for Christmas?" J.B. said, in his best imitation of what a Santa should sound like.

"I really, really, really..."

"FINSTER!"

"Sorry, J.B. I want a red flyer wagon with white sidewalls."

"What? What kind of a boy are you, anyway? Nobody has wagons anymore. Wagons are for sissies. Boys have miniature cars, and skateboards and electric trains. And don't you know that space exploration is really big this year? What you real need is one of these life sized, rubberized, cute and cuddly, squeaks when you squeeze him, fantastic space alien doll with a red heart light. Batteries not included."

"Okay, J.B."

"You see," J.B. said as he jumped to his feet, dumping Finster to the floor. "That's how it's done. See to it that you follow the manual at all times."

"Why do you want to push the space alien doll?" One of the Santas asked.

"Economics, my friend, economics. We bought them for $1.32 each, they retail at $12.95 and we're runnin' them squeaky little suckers at $10.95. We'll make a killing on the batteries, too. We got 149 cases of those stupid looking outer space rubber duckies crammed in the warehouse. Gotta move 'em out."

"But, J.B." Finster spoke up. "That movie left town a long time ago and since then we can't give those bug-eyed battery burners away."

"Right, so we gotta push 'em. Creative marketing, that's the key. The American way. Remember when we got stuck with those flying saucer things from that other movie a few years back?"

"Flying saucer things?" One of the Santas asked.

"Yes. Flying saucer things. Finster, you remember that movie, don't you?"

"Yes, J.B." Finster didn't, exactly. But he wasn't about to let J.B. know.

"Do you remember how we got rid of them?"

"Yes, J.B. I mean, no J.B. I guess I don't remember.'"

"You gotta do something about your memory, boy. We knocked the lights off, painted them different colors and sold them as Frisbees. What a hassle and we only made $6.00 on each one. Not this time."

"Yes, J.B."

"No, J.B."

"Right, J.B."

"Alright, then, Get busy and sell some toys. I want to hear those cash registers ringing. You all know your quotas and remember...I'LL BE WATCHING!"

"Yes, J.B." Everyone answered.   *"It's gonna be a tough*

Christmas," J.B. thought as he left.

****

"...and besides, Mr. Mayor," Councilman Archibald had caught up with the Mayor just as he was about to enter the courthouse. He wasted no time in letting him know how he felt about the current problem. "The Nativity scene is a tradition and a symbol of...:"

"I know it's a symbol, Archie..." The Mayor tried to get a word in edgewise. Not easy with the Councilman at any time, and even worse when he was wound up, like he was this morning.

"...the true meaning of the reason why all civilized people..."

"Archie, we've been through all this..."

"...gather at this time."

"Good morning Mr. Mayor, Councilman Archibald." Jane Boyce, the Mayor's secretary, greeted the two men as they entered the office.

"Good morning, Jane." The Mayor answered.

Councilman Archibald stopped in mid sentence and flashed his biggest politician grin as he surveyed the office. Along with secretary Boyce were two clerks at their desks to the right of the door, and Sam Barns, the building custodian emptying the wastebaskets into a large rolling trashcan.

"Good morning public servants. It is sooo good to see you at your posts so early this morning. The taxpayers of this fair city would be pleased, as I am, with your dedication. And furthermore..."

"Archie." The Mayor cut him off. "Cut out the campaign speech and get in here. The election isn't until next year."

"Right, Mr. Mayor." Archie mumbled as he followed the Mayor into his office.

"And, Jane?"

"Yes, Mr. Mayor."

"Hold all my calls until I'm through with Archie."

"Will do, good luck."

"Uh huh." G.D. knew just what she was talking about. He entered the office and closed the door behind him.

"Well, the Councilman is in rare form this morning." Jim Walker, the senior clerk in the office looked up from his desk. "What a windbag."

"Doesn't he ever shut up?" Asked Paul Moore, the other clerk.

"Hardly ever. His wife tells me he even talks in his sleep." Jane answered.

"Then she shouldn't have any trouble falling asleep. He can

render an entire room full of people unconscious in less than five minutes with one of his speeches."

"Right, best cure for insomnia that ever was."

"How can a man talk so long and still say nothin'." Asked Sam. "I don't know how the Mayor can put up with it. It would drive me nuts."

"Only if you stayed awake." Jim laughed as he made his way to the coffee pot located on a small table behind Jane's desk. "And this thing with the Nativity Scene has really pushed his buttons."

"His, and everybody else in this town with an ax to grind." Jane answered as she reached for the phone. "Good morning, Mayor's Office. How may I direct your call?"

"I love it when she does that." Jim whispered. "There's nobody else working here except the Mayor, the three of us and Sam. And he doesn't even have a phone."

"And I thank the Good Lord for that blessing." Sam answered as he started out of the office.

"See you hard working public servants later."

"I'm sorry, the Mayor is in a meeting right now, can I take a message?" Jane pulled a small notepad from her desk drawer as she spoke. "I know it's important J.B., I mean Mr. Nickels, but he asked that we hold all his calls."

"What do you suppose he wants?" Jim sat down at his desk and took a sip of his coffee.

"Probably wants the Mayor to reconsider his offer of the new Nativity Scene." Paul answered.

"Oh yeah, the really fancy one with all the lights and the animals that moved."

"That's would be the one."

"Wasn't that pretty expensive?"

"Well, J.B. was gonna give us a discount if we put it in his storefront window."

"How much of a discount?"

"He was only gonna charge us about a hundred percent over his cost."

"What a deal." Paul and Jim started laughing when Jane made a face that quieted them down.

"Will you two cut it out?" She whispered, with her hand over the mouthpiece on the phone. "I can't hear a thing."

"Okay, okay." The two clerks chuckled softly. "We'll be good."

"Yes sir, I'll have him call you just as soon as he is free." Jane hung up the phone. "Every time J.B. calls he keeps him on the phone forever. Sometimes I think he talks more than Councilman

Archibald."

"Impossible."

"Not really. Every time he calls I feel like I'm talking to one of those telephone solicitors that always call around dinnertime. Everything he says is a sales pitch."

"I saw him talking to his new crop of Santa's at the store." Paul looked up from his desk. "It was the most degrading thing I ever saw. And this year's crop of Santa's looks even worse than last year."

"Well, what do you expect? With the money he pays them those guys from the homeless shelter are the only ones who ever apply."

"Right, and it seems they never apply two years in a row."

"Would you?"

"Nope."

"You know who else called yesterday." Jane asked.

"Could be anybody, the way this town's getting."

"Councilman Humble's wife."

"Oh no. What did she want?"

"Said she was getting a group of ladies together to picket the Nativity Scene."

"What? Why? No, wait a minute, don't tell me. I heard Eloise Simonet at the meeting last night. And since Bertha is planning on being the next president of W.H.E.N. then I'll bet she's calling about equal representation in the cradle?"

"That, too. But she was really up in arms because there didn't seem to be any equal representation among the animals. You know, equal numbers of male and female." Jane rolled her eyes. "And, on top of that, Mayor Johnson, I mean ex-Mayor Johnson, called to tell the Mayor just what he would do in this situation."

"I'll bet that was fun."

"Well, the Mayor was at lunch so I took a message. He wanted to let G.D. know that this was what he gets for winning the election."

"He always was a nice guy."

"Yeah, right. A real great human being."

"You know," Jane said. "There is one positive thing about this whole situation."

"Really, and just what might that be?"

"When have so many people been so interested in what goes on at City Hall?"

The three sat quietly for a moment before Paul looked up. "Yeah, and when has the Mayor ever had a chance to do something really big?"

"Big?"

"Big enough for this town. Looks like it's up to him to decide if we're gonna forget Christmas."

****

"Have a seat, Archie." The Mayor said as he closed the door to his office. "And hold the campaign speeches. I need to run something by you."

"Right, Mr. Mayor."

"Archie, we've known each other since kindergarten." The Mayor said as he sat down at his desk. "And, even though you have a tendency to be long winded..."

"Excuse me?" Archie sat up in the chair.

"...You know I respect your viewpoint on most things." G.D. continued, ignoring the question. "So I want to spend some time just looking at a few things that are important, for us, and this town."

Archie sat back in the chair and looked around the office. Besides the large desk in front of the window there were two chairs facing it, one of which Archie sat in, a small bookcase on the left wall and a file cabinet in the corner. A large picture of Colonel Rufus Newton hung on the wall opposite the desk and was the only picture in the room except for a framed photo of the Mayor and his family on top of the bookcase. *"This office sure looks like G.D."* Archie thought. *"No nonsense."*

"You know, " the Mayor began. "We've lived in this town all our lives, except for a couple of years in the Army, and I don't know about you but I have fond memories of what Christmas used to be around here."

"Yes, so do I. Seems sad to see it today." Archie's politician bluster was gone. Now these were just two old friends talking about something that was important to both of them.

"For as long as the Mill has been here that Nativity Scene has been the focus and centerpiece of Christmas for Newton's Mill."

"Do you remember," Archie smiled at the thought. "When the whole town gathered at the Mill on Christmas Eve?"

"And all the Churches in town got together and sang carols around the set."

"And everybody joined in. Even the ones who couldn't carry a tune."

"You had to bring that up, didn't you." The Mayor laughed.

"Sorry, G.D." Archie was laughing, too.

"It was what Christmas was all about. The carols, the snow..."

"Yeah, we had snow almost every year." Archie added.

"...And all the kids excited about getting home so they could get the milk and cookies out for Santa." G.D. continued. "Even the big kids that knew the truth about Santa."

"Those were great times, G.D. Before the Mill closed."

G.D. and Archie sat silently, lost in thoughts of better times.

"What happened, Archie?" The Mayor spoke softly. "How did we get to this place?"

Archie didn't answer right away, just sat looking out the window. It was a question he had asked himself more than once. "I don't know. Maybe it was when all those folks started buying up the farmland and building houses. They brought a lot of big city ideas with them."

"Big city ideas are okay, I guess. We're not a small town anymore. But some of our small town ideas are okay, too. And it might be unfair to put all this on to them. Some of them are good folks."

"I think most of them are. It's just a few that cause trouble. But they would cause trouble anywhere, I guess."

"Anyway. I have to decide how to vote on the matter. But it sure seems to be a bigger problem than it ought to be. Everything's changing."

"Not everything, G.D." Archie said as he stood to leave. "It's snowing."

****

While Archie and the Mayor were discussing the state of things the Mayor's secretary had been fielding several phone calls. And now every hold button on the phone was blinking. "I'll bet every one of these calls is about the same thing." Jane said as the door to the Mayor's office opened.

"I'll be going now, Mr. Mayor." Archie had dropped back into his politician mode. "I must be about my business. There are so many things awaiting my attention. Continue your efforts dedicated public servants."

"Oh, we will, Councilman Archibald. We will." Jim said as he looked up from his desk.

"Splendid, splendid. Then I shall be on my way."

"Have a good day, Archie." The Mayor called from his office.

"Thank you, Mr. Mayor. You, too."

"Jane," G.D. called to his secretary as Archie closed the door behind him. "Every light on my phone is blinking. Are there that many people waiting to talk to me."

"I'm afraid so, Mr. Mayor. Plus a few I didn't have room for."

"Do I need to ask what they want to talk about?"

"I think you already know." June said.

"Yeah, right. Okay, who has been waiting the longest?"

"Just start with the first one on the left and work your way to the right."

"That sounds easy." G.D. said as he came from behind the desk and walked to the door. "I'll close this door so you don't hear my pain."

"Good luck, Mr. Mayor." Paul said from his desk.

"Thanks, I think." G.D. laughed as he closed the door.

The Mayor went back to his desk, took a deep breath and punched the first button. "Hello, this is the Mayor."

"Mr. Mayor, this is the Fire Chief."

"Yes, Chief, what is it?"

"It's time for the monthly fire drill."

"The monthly fired drill? Does that have to be done today?"

"This is the week for it."

"Well, can't you do it on Saturday?" G.D. took a look at the blinking lights on his phone.

"Things are busy around here today."

"But there's nobody at work on Saturday."

"Exactly, that's why I suggested it."

"But, Mr. Mayor, if we do it on Saturday there won't be any way to make sure the employees there follow the rules."

"Chief, there are only four of us working in this building and we are all in the same office. How tough can that be?"

"City and County Regulation 7745-3116, Section 1004, subsection 345, paragraph 3, states that fire drills are to be conducted during working hours in order..."

"Okay, Chief, okay." The Mayor interrupted. "Do it whenever you want. I've got several more calls to answer so hold off for awhile."

"Right, Mr. Mayor. Will do. Goodbye."

"Goodbye, Chief." G.D. punched the next button, no one there. *"Must have got tired of waiting,"* he thought as he pushed the third button."

"Hello, this is the Mayor."

"Mr. Mayor, Reverend Brown here."

"Oh, good morning Artemis. What's up?" the Mayor answered. "As if I didn't know." He whispered to himself.

"What was that?"

"I said it looks like we're getting some snow."

"Oh, that it does, that it does. I suppose you have an idea why I'm calling."

"Wouldn't have anything to do with last night's council meeting would it?"

"You see, that's why you're such a good Mayor. You're aware of your community and it's concerns."

"Thanks for the compliment, Artemis. But it wasn't too tough to figure out since that's all that anybody seems to want to talk about."

"And I'm no exception, G.D. Some of what was said last night was disgraceful. I can't believe that our town has come to this."

"Artemis, I understand your concerns. Christmas is important to you and every other Church in town. But you have to understand that there is more at stake here."

"I know G.D., seems like everybody has their own ideas of what Christmas is all about."

"Archie and I were just talking this morning about how Christmas was a lot different back when the Mill was open."

"Oh yes, those were good days. Gone now, though."

"I'm afraid so. Listen, Artemis, I know you and the other clergymen in town are concerned about this whole Nativity Scene thing. Let me just assure you that I won't make any hasty decisions until I've had some time to think this all through."

"Well, I guess we can't ask for more than that. And knowing you as I do I'm confident that it will be the right one. We will be praying for you. So long."

"So long, Artemis, and thanks for the prayers." The Mayor hung up the phone. There were still three buttons blinking. *"Two down, three to go."* He thought as he pushed the next button.

****

"I don't know why I let her treat me that way." Hebert Humble thought as he sat at his kitchen table with an almost cold cup of coffee. He hadn't been able to sleep after the Council meeting. And Bertha didn't make it any easier on him. From the time they left the meeting and until she finally went up to bed, she continued to berate him for almost voting for the Nativity Scene.

"I should stand up for myself. Make my own decisions. I'm a man." Hebert's thoughts continued. *"And besides, the Nativity Scene is a big part of Christmas around here. So, why is Bertha so set against it?"*

"Hebert!!!" It was Bertha calling from the bedroom. "Where are you?"

"Here, in the kitchen." Hebert called. "I couldn't sleep." Bertha came to the door of the kitchen. "Couldn't sleep, eh? Well, no wonder. Your conscience should be really bothering you about what you almost did. I simply cannot

understand why you would embarrass me in front of the entire town."

"But..." Hebert tried to answer.

"You know that I'm in line for the Presidency of W.H.E.N. and just how would it look if my husband voted for something W.H.E.N. is against? Honestly, Hebert, I don't know what you were thinking."

"But..." He tried again.

"I have an image to uphold here, Hebert. And if you continue in your attempts to embarrass me in public it will mean a serious problem in our marriage. Do you understand?"

"Yes, dear." Hebert gave up. He never could argue with Bertha. Even when they were kids growing up she was always the strong one. She set her eyes on Hebert and he didn't stand a chance. Bertha saw in Hebert an easily controlled, gentle person who wouldn't be difficult to handle. So as soon as they were old enough she informed him that they were getting married, that was that, and he had no choice in the matter. "Yes dear" was his answer then, too.

"Now," Bertha continued. "I have a very full schedule for today. Meetings with the members of W.H.E.N. to discuss my Presidency, and an afternoon of shopping at J.B. Nickels. After all, the President of such a prestigious organization as W.H.E.N. can't be seen in just any old rags, now can she?"

"No, dear." Hebert mumbled. When dealing with Bertha it was best to keep your answers simple. Yes or no usually worked fine.

"I have a few things for you to do around the house today."

"But..." Hebert just knew this was going to one of those days.

"Before you leave for work I need the garbage taken out, the house vacuumed and the kitchen tidied up. And I'm sure that coffee is ice cold. Get rid of it and put the cup in the dishwasher."

"Yes..." He didn't even get the 'dear' out.

"When you get home from work I want you to clean out the garage. It's just full of those silly tools you never use. I don't care what you do with them. Just get them out of there. I will need lots of room for the literature and other supplies from W.H.E.N. and the garage is the best place. Leave room for my car, but you can park yours in the driveway. It's older than mine, anyway."

Hebert didn't even try to answer. It wouldn't have done any good anyway. When Bertha got wound up there was no stopping her. And she was really rolling. She gave him several more directions then started back to the bedroom. "And don't forget," she called over her shoulder. "Today is the W.H.E.N. meeting. I may be home late."

"The later the better." Hebert mumbled.

"What!!!" Bertha had heard him.

"I said I need to pick up some butter." He called.

"Well, get it when you go to the store for all the other stuff you have to get for the dinner party tonight."

"Dinner party?" Hebert didn't know anything about any dinner party.

"Yes, dinner party. I've invited the leaders of all the groups opposed to the Nativity Scene to dinner and a discussion of a plan of action." Bertha shouted from the bedroom. "I told you about it yesterday."

"I don't think so." Hebert answered. "I don't remember you saying anything about it."

Bertha suddenly appeared in the doorway, her face an angry red. She had forgotten to tell Hebert about it but she wasn't going to admit she could have forgotten. "Hebert. You have the worst memory in the world. I distinctly told you that we were having a dinner party for twelve people tonight. That's why you need to go to the market today."

"I don't..."

"I know you don't. You never do. The list of stuff you need is on the refrigerator door. Don't forget anything." And Bertha turned and stormed back into the bedroom, leaving Hebert alone with his thoughts.

"I don't know when I'm supposed to find time to do all this today." He thought. Hebert ran a bookstore in the J.B. Nickels department store promenade. With all these chores and now the grocery shopping he would have to let his clerk, Katie handle the store today. She was a good worker and he was very glad he hired her. She was like a daughter to him, and since Bertha had told him from the very beginning that there would be no children, he treated her like the daughter he never had. *"I'm lucky to have such a capable clerk. Sure wish I could afford to pay her more money."* But that wasn't likely, since Hebert opened the store with money from his wife's parents, Bertha also controlled the business with an iron hand. And raises for anyone, including Hebert, were out of the question.

But the bookstore was Hebert's refuge. When things were bad with Bertha, which was most of the time, he could always find comfort in the quiet orderliness of the store. And he had many loyal customers who had shopped there for years. He would have been surprised to know that most of them shopped there because of their affection for him and the friendships that he had cultivated over the years. Bertha may not have cared much for Hebert, but there were a lot of folks in Newton's Mill that did.

"Haven't you started cleaning up this kitchen, yet?" Bertha swept in from the bedroom like a tornado. She was dressed and ready to leave but she didn't want to miss one more chance to give Hebert a hard time. It was, unfortunately for him, her one real enjoyment in life. "Quit daydreaming and get busy." And with that she was out the door and gone.   Hebert got up slowly from the table and began cleaning up the kitchen. As he did he remembered the words to an old song, *"Tote that barge, lift that bale..."* and he thought. *"It's a good thing there aren't any of those things here or she would have me doing that, too."*

****

"Two down, three to go," G.D. thought as he punched the next button on his phone. "Mayor Steward. Oh, hello Helen, what's up?"

"How's the morning going, G.D.?" Helen seldom called him at work but she knew how much pressure he was under and it worried her. "Anything exciting going on?"

"Exciting, why sure, my whole day is just one exciting thing after another. Just this morning I had a phone call from Artemis about the meeting last night. And Archie waylaid me on the way in and we spent a few minutes discussing the situation."

"Only a few minutes?" Helen laughed. "How did you manage that?"

"Interesting thing about Archie, when I get him alone, without his constituents around, he is just old Nate Archibald that's been my friend for, must be a hundred years. Seems he can turn it on and off like a faucet."

"Well, if you say so. Anything else?"

"Oh, right, and the Fire Chief called and wants to schedule a fire drill to test our evacuation plan."

"Evacuation plan? There's only four of you working there, how hard can it be?"

"Exactly what I told him, word for word in fact, but he quoted me Chapter and verse of the State Fire Regulations so I guess we will be having a fire drill any minute now. I've got two more calls waiting. Was there something you wanted?"

"Yes, I need a couple of things from the store on your way home tonight."

"Right, just let me get something to write on. Okay, shoot."

"Get a loaf of bread, you know the kind I like, a gallon of milk, two pounds of hamburger and some bananas."

"Okay, got it. A loaf of bread, the kind you like, milk, hamburger and bananas. That's gonna make some sandwich.

Should I pick up some bicarbonate, too?"

"Very funny, G.D.. At least you haven't lost your sense of humor."

"Not yet, anyway. Love ya. Bye." G.D. punched the next blinking button.

"Mayor Steward. Oh, Hello John. What can I do for you?" It was John Knot, owner of the local lumberyard.

"Mr. Mayor, I was at the Council meeting last night." John began.

"How did I know?" the mayor mumbled.

"Excuse me?"

"I said it's looking like snow. What can I do for you, John?"

"Well, as you know I run the biggest lumber yard and building material store in this whole county, maybe even the whole state, the jury is still out on that one."

"Yes John, I know. They don't call you Mr. Lumber for nothing."

"That's right, that's right." John laughed his big booming laugh. Everything about John was big. His lumberyard, his house, his truck and even himself. Everything that is except for his wife Peggy. She was all of about five feet tall and thin as a rail. The

Knot's had six kids, all boys, but Peggy still looked like she did that day twenty years ago when she and John first tied the knot. In fact, "tying the knots" has been a standing joke around town ever since.

"Anyway, Mr. Mayor, after the meeting last night Peggy and I talked it over and decided we wanted to do something special. So we're gonna donate enough lumber and materials to build a stable for the Nativity Scene. Should make it look real authentic."

"Well, that's great, John. But you know the decision about the Nativity Scene hasn't been made yet."

"Oh, I know that, G.D. but I just thought if folks knew we could have a real authentic looking Nativity Scene then they might all agree that it's the right thing to do."

"That's a great idea, John. But I don't think the authenticity of the Nativity Scene is the problem here. This whole question is a lot bigger than that, I think. But I really appreciate the offer."

"Okay, Mr. Mayor, you're probably right. Just remember the offer, if you need it."

"I will, John, and thanks. Say hello to Peggy for me."

"Will do, you do the same to Helen for me. So long."

"So long, John." The Mayor hung up the phone and sat looking at the last blinking light on his phone. *"Do I really want to answer this?"* He thought. *"Oh well, it's getting close to lunch, maybe I can make it fast."* He picked up the receiver and punched the last button "This is the Mayor."

"Well, finally," came the indignant voice of Bertha Humble. "Surely the Mayor of a town the size of Newton's Mill could manage to answer his phone a little more promptly."

"Oh, Hello, Bertha. Sorry about the wait. It's busy around here." G.D. made his voice sound pleasant, although a phone call from Bertha never turned out to be anything but trouble.

"Really? You politicians are all alike. Never care about the little people who got you elected."

"Bertha, for one thing I don't think of myself as a politician, and for another thing you're not one of the "little people" of this town and I know for a fact that you didn't vote for me in the last election. You told me so yourself. Now what can I do for you?"

In spite of his efforts there was a hard edge to G.D.'s answer and Bertha could hear it. While she took pleasure in belittling Hebert and being generally nasty to most everyone, she was a little afraid of the Mayor. She knew him to be a strong man, with a great sense of fairness. Qualities that she found herself unable to deal with. Some of the harshness went out of her voice.

"Mr. Mayor, as you may know I have been nominated for the Presidency of the local chapter of Women Hoping For Equality

Now."

"Yes, I had heard something to that effect."

"Well, in honor of that nomination I am having a dinner party at my home this evening for the members of the local chapter. We will be gathering input on the latest crisis of our town."

"The what?"

"The latest crisis here in our town."

"And that would be?" The Mayor knew what she was talking about but he wanted to hear it from her.

"The question of the Nativity Scene, of course."

"Excuse me, Bertha, but I'm sure if you looked around you could find at least a dozen things more critical than this Nativity Scene."

"I'm not sure you quite understand the situation here." Bertha continued. "This is a subject that has polarized our community. Why everyone from the most important people in town right down to the simple folk are concerned about it."

"I wonder how many of the simple folk you know." mumbled the Mayor.

"I'm sorry, what did you say?" Bertha asked.

"I said I think it might be going to snow." The Mayor answered.

"Oh, right, it does look that way. But that is beside the point. I would like you to attend my dinner party tomorrow so that we can bring you up to speed on our feeling regarding this matter."

"Up to speed, eh?" The Mayor chuckled, in spite of himself. "I don't think that would be such a good idea."

"And just why not?" Bertha asked, haughtily.

"Because if I go to your dinner party then I will have to attend every rally, luncheon, gathering and meeting of every group with an interest in the problem. And you will all be trying to influence my vote."

"But, Mr. Mayor..."

"That's it, Bertha. Have your dinner party and discuss whatever you want to discuss but it will have to be without me. I have to go now. Thanks for calling." And before Bertha could answer G.D. hung up the phone.

****

Meanwhile, back at the J.B. Nickels Department Store and Shopping Mall, one of the successful Santa candidates was about to get his "baptism of fire." Otherwise known as his first day in the chair. This ritual was known to strike fear in the hearts of many a strong man. Facing the onslaught of literally hundreds of pushing, shoving, squirming little kids eager to fill Santa in on their desires for Christmas toys was bad enough, but the hovering presence of J.B. Nickels elevated the whole experience to a level of severe emotional trauma.

And now, into that situation walked Seamus McGillicudy.

The screams that erupted from the children waiting in line as he made his entrance from the dressing room almost caused him to turn and run. Unfortunately for him, his escape was blocked by J.B. Nickels' newly promoted assistant Harold Finster. Finster's hand was placed firmly between McGillicudy's shoulder blades and he had a strong grip on his arm as he guided him past the now frantic children to the throne-like Santa seat.

"Remember, McGillicudy," Finster whispered, ominously, as he pushed him down into the chair. *"J.B. is watching."*

Taking a deep breath, as Finster turned to leave, McGillicudy spoke to one of the two young girls who were Santa's Elves, "Okay, bring 'em on." He tried to sound confident and in control but the panic in his voice caused the girl to smile. She had seen it all before.

"I'll bet he doesn't get through the day." She thought.

Santa's area sat right in the center of the large open space almost directly across from J.B. Nickels store. To one side was the Food Court, to the other a line of shops selling items not carried in the department store. That was one of the conditions of opening a store in the Mall. You couldn't compete with anything that J.B. sold in his store. So stores came and went on a regular basis. Just behind Santa's chair was a small bench where folks could sit and watch the crowds, eat a snack from the food court, or just catch a minute's rest. Sitting on the bench, out of sight of J.B.'s office window, was the tall man from the group of Santa possibilities of the morning. From his position he could easily hear the children as they spoke to Santa.

The first child climbed up on Santa's lap, stepping on his toe and reaching for his beard. "Ho-ho-ho," McGilligudy boomed, in his best Santa voice while grabbing the kid's hand to keep him from yanking off the beard. "And what big expensive toy do you want for Christmas?"

"Gee, Santa, I really, really, really want a red flyer wagon with white sidewalls." The kid fairly screamed.

McGillicudy couldn't believe his ears. It was just like the academy. *"This is gonna be a cinch."* He thought.

"Well," came a voice from behind the seat. "They are having a great sale on those down at Farnsworth's Hardware Store. And they're only $19.95."

"Wow, thanks, Santa." The young boy cried as he jumped off Santa's lap. "C'mon, Mom, they got a sale on those wagons down at Farnsworth's."

McGillicudy looked around. "Where did that come from?"

"Here's the next child, Santa." The young girl Elf said. "And you better be careful,

J. B. is watching."

"I know, I know." McGillicudy said. "Ho-Ho-Ho, and just what big expensive toy..."

"Well," the kid interrupted. "I wanted one of those red flyer wagons too but now that I know Farnsworth's is selling them I guess, I would like a train set."

"A train set?" McGillicudy laughed. "That's a pretty good..."

"They have train sets on special at Farnsworth's, too" Came the same voice as before. "And they're cheaper than what Nickel's sells them for."

"Alright!" yelled the kid. "Thanks Santa, you're the greatest. C'mon Mom, Farnsworth's is selling the train sets, on sale." The boy shouted as he grabbed his mother by the hand, pulling her along toward the exit

"What are you doing?" The young girl Elf whispered in McGillicudy's ear. *"I told you that J.B. was watching."*

"Me?" McGillicudy said. "I didn't do anything. Didn't you hear the voice?"

"Oh boy," the girl thought. *"It's happening quicker than I expected. He's cracking already."*

Suddenly, J.B. Nickels appeared at the door of his store. His face was red, his hands were clenched at his sides as he stood watching Santa.

"Now you've done it," the Elf warned. "J.B.'s on the warpath."

"Quick," McGillicudy whispered. *"Get another kid up here."*

The Elf grabbed the arm of the next kid, a little girl, and almost threw her on Santa's lap.

With one eye on J.B. McGillicudy asked the girl. "Now, what big expensive toy do you want for Christmas?"

"Well, Santa, I really, really, really want..." The girl began.

"A Red Flyer wagon with white sidewalls?" McGillicudy interrupted.

"No, Santa, I want one of those Space Alien dolls that lights up."

"Huh?"

"Yeah, Santa. I want one of the Space Alien Dolls. I really like outer space stuff."

"Farnsworth has telescopes on sale." Came the same voice as before. "You can see stars and planets and everything."

"Gee, Santa," The little girl squealed. "That's even better than one of those dolls. Hey Mom, Santa says Farnsworth's is having a sale on telescopes."

"Where's Farnsworth's?"' The girl's mother asked.

"Just follow those other kids." Santa said, as he slumped back in his chair.

J.B. Nickels stormed past the line of kids and, with his face just inches away from

McGillicudy's, growled. "Just what do you think you are doing?"

"But." McGillicudy started.

"But what? You're sending all the kids to Farnsworth's."

"It's not me," pleaded McGillicudy. "Someone keeps saying these things."

"Someone?"

"Yes, it sounds like it's coming from behind the chair here."

"Behind the chair?" J.B. snarled, as he stepped around the side to look behind it. There was no one on the bench. "There's nobody back here."

"But."

"I said there's nobody back here." J.B. stormed back around the chair. "YOU ARE FIRED."

"Fired? But J.B."

"I said you're fired. Turn in your suit." J.B. yanked McGillicudy to his feet.

As J.B. dragged the hapless Santa towards the dressing room the young girl Elf placed an "Out To Lunch" sign on the chair.

"Let's get some lunch," she said to the other girl Elf.

****

G.D. sat staring at the phone for a minute, hoping it wouldn't ring again. *"This whole Nativity Scene thing is getting totally out of hand."* He thought as he stood and headed for the door of his office. *"I can't remember anything else that has split this town the way this has. And I really am not comfortable being the final say in the situation. Oh well, it's almost lunchtime. Maybe I'll be able to think better on a full stomach."*

He stood for a moment with his hand on the knob. *"Can't let the Jayne and the clerks see how this thing has me spooked."* He forced a smile as he opened the door.

"Well, Mr. Mayor, I see you survived all those calls." Jayne said as he came out of his office.

"Yes, barely." He laughed. And then in his best impersonation of Councilman Archibald's campaign voice he warned them, "By the way, dedicated public servants, we're about to have a fire drill."

"A what?" Walker asked.

"A fire drill. Any minute now."

"What do we need a fire drill for?" The other clerk wanted to know. "There's only four of us in this office. How hard can that be?"

"Exactly what I told the chief when he called. Word for word."

"You couldn't talk him out of it?" Jayne asked.

"I tried. But he quoted me all these paragraphs and responsibilities from the State Fire Safety Code, and I was stuck."

"Why doesn't he just have it on Saturday, when there's nobody here?"

"I made that suggestion, too."

"And?"

"No soap. It's today. But I have an idea."

"What's that, Mr. Mayor?" asked Sam Barnes as he came into the office with an empty trashcan.

"Let's break for lunch."

"Now there's a great idea." Paul Moore agreed. "And if we

hurry we can be out of here before Chief Stovall has a chance to do anything."

"What are we talking about?" Sam said, looking around the office. "Chief Stovall wants to have a fire drill."

"A fire drill? There's only..."

"We know." Jayne interrupted. "There's only four of us in the office."

"Five if you count me." Corrected Sam. "How hard can it be?"

The Mayor, Jayne, Jim and Paul all looked at each other and then broke into laughter.

"What's so funny?" Sam wanted to know.

"We all said the same thing." The Mayor told him.

"Well," Sam joined in the laughter. "Great minds do think alike."

"Let's get out of here." The Mayor said as he started for the door.

The five of them left the office, walked out the front door and stood for a moment.

"Are you going home for lunch, Mr. Mayor?" Jayne asked.

"No, I think I'm going over to Charlie's and have a salad. I need some time to think. What are you all going to do?"

"I guess we're all going to the Pizza Palace. They're having a special on peanut butter pizza."

"What? Peanut Butter Pizza?" The Mayor stared at Jayne. "You can't be serious?"

"Just kidding, Mr. Mayor. You looked like you could use a laugh."

"Does it show that much?"

"Yeah. A little bit." Paul told him. "But you do have one positive thing here."

"And that would be?"

"When have so many people been so interested in what went on at City Hall?"

"If you say so. I'll see you after lunch." The Mayor turned and walked away.

****

It was just a short walk from City Hall to Charlie's but as G.D. was walking along a young boy fell in step with him.

"Hey, Mr. Mayor." The boy spoke. "Where you headed?"

"Oh, hello Spike." The Mayor recognized Bob Morgan's ten-year-old son. "Just going over to Charlie's to get lunch. How are you?"

"I'm good, Mr. Mayor but I got a question for you."

"Shoot."

"You gonna let us have Christmas this year?"

"What?"

"Are you gonna let us have Christmas this year?"

"Why wouldn't we have Christmas this year?"

"Well, my Dad says it's up to you whether we have it or not."

Now, G.D. had known Spike's Dad for more than twenty years. And sometimes they didn't always see things quite the same way. But he couldn't believe that Bob could have told his son there wasn't going to be Christmas this year.

"Well, Mr. Mayor?" Spike asked. But before he had a chance to respond several other young boys and girls joined Spike.

"Whatcha doin' Spike?" One of them asked.

"I'm discussin' Christmas with the Mayor. Only he ain't talkin'"

"Now just a minute..."

"Did ya ask him if we're gonna have Christmas this year?" One of the children spoke up.

"Yeah," another child joined in. "How about it, Mr. Mayor? Are you gonna let us have Christmas this year?"

"Listen kids, you have the wrong idea about this." The Mayor explained.

"Oh yeah?" Spike asked. "That's what you say."

"No, listen..." The Mayor tried to speak but the questions came too fast for him to answer.

"I want a new bike for Christmas, but thanks to you I probably won't get it."

"My folks say that if we don't have Christmas this year it'll be all your fault."

"So, what are you gonna say to everybody when we don't have Christmas?'

"Yeah. It's a big time in a kid's life. And thanks to you it's not gonna happen. I can see it all now. Lot's of unhappy kids because you wouldn't let them have Christmas."

"C'mon, Mr. Mayor. You gonna spoil it for all us kids?"

"Listen kids, " The Mayor tried to get a word in but it was no use. The kids kept after him.

"I read about this mean guy named Scrooge who hated

Christmas. Is he any relation to you?

"I'll bet you had Christmas when you were a kid. So how come you don't want us to have it?"

"Yeah, Mr. Mayor, Why don't you just let Christmas alone?"

"My Sister wants a doll. That's not much to ask. But I guess she won't get it, thanks to you."

"All right, you kids," It was Councilman Archibald, to the rescue. "What's going on here?"

"We're just tryin' to find out why the Mayor won't let us have Christmas this year." Spike Morgan answered, as he seemed to be the spokesman for the group.

"Well, just a moment now, I think your going a bit too far." Archie spoke in his Councilman voice, hoping to impress the kids. "The Mayor isn't going to stop you from having Christmas."

"Oh yeah," Spike answered. "Well, my Dad says if we don't have Christmas this year it's gonna be all his fault."

"That's right," Several of the other kids chimed in. "It's all his fault. It's all his fault."

"Enough!" Archie was getting a little upset. "The Mayor has better things to do than sit here and be subjected to this sort of attack."

"We're not attacking him," Spoke a girl from the back of the crowd of children. "We just want some answers."

"How about it, Mr. Mayor?" Spike spoke. "Got any answers for us?"

G.D. sat silent for a moment, trying to gather his thoughts.

"That's what I thought." Spike said as he turned to the crowd of kids. "He's got nothin' to say. C'mon, let's go."

And with that the kids headed off down the street, leaving G.D. and Archie watching them go.

"This whole thing is getting out of hand." Archie spoke without looking at the Mayor. "Too many people have too much to say about it."

"I know, Archie, and I think it's only gonna get worse before the meeting next Tuesday."

"Well, I'm behind you 100 percent. You know that."

"Thanks. And thanks for bailing me out with those kids."

"My pleasure, Mr. Mayor."

"Want to get some lunch?"

"No, it's a bit too early for me. Say, isn't it a bit too early for you, as well?"

"Yeah, but Chief Stovall wanted to have a fire drill at City Hall."

"A fire drill?"

"Yeah, he wanted to test the evacuation plan."

"Wait a minute. Isn't there just four of you in the office?"

"That's right."

"So, how hard can it be?"

"Exactly what I told him, word for word." The Mayor stood up. "So we instituted our own evacuation plan and left for lunch early."

"A wise decision. See you later, G.D."

"So long, Archie, and thanks again."

****

While the Mayor was on the hot seat being grilled by the kids J.B. Nickels was hot under the collar because of his pitiful crop of Santas. He had stormed back to his office after practically throwing the half dressed, hapless Santa out of the store.

"Get another Santa on that chair right now!" He yelled at Finster as he slammed the door. He was not in a good frame of mind.

"I think these sorry excuses for Santa's get more miserable every year." He spoke out loud, although there was no one else in the office. "At this rate we will wind up with so much stuff left over after Christmas we won't be able to give it away." He shuddered at the thought. "I don't know why I can't start Christmas in June. There's just not enough time between Thanksgiving and Christmas to sell all the stuff we have.

J.B. walked over to the huge oak desk that dominated his office, picked up a handful of papers, and sorted through them. "Look at these." He growled. "Invoices for all the Christmas items we brought in, at really low prices, so we could sell them at really high prices. But if business doesn't pick up pretty soon I'm gonna be stuck with a lot of cheap stuff that no one will want."

He threw the papers down on the desk as someone knocked on the door.

"Who is it?" He yelled. "And where's my secretary?"

"On the other side of this door." Came the answer.

"Oh." J.B. calmed down. You see, his secretary was his wife. And if there was anyone tougher than J.B. Nickels, it was Cora Nickels. Tough on J.B. anyway. "What is it, dear?"

The door opened and Cora came in.

Now, some people just enter a room. But Cora? Well, she

usually attacked a room when she entered.

"Who are you talking to in here, J.B.?" She said, looking around the room.

"No one, dear. Just myself."

"Just yourself? Well, that must have been an interesting conversation." Cora was not intimidated by her husband's power. "And what gem of wisdom did you share with yourself?"

"Oh, nothing, dear." Came the meek reply. "I just had to fire another Santa, and I was thinking how nice it would be if we could start Christmas in June."

"June!"

"Yes, just think of how much merchandise we could sell if we started the Christmas Season that early."

"J.B., we've pushed the season nearly to Halloween now. People aren't gonna be thinking about Christmas when it's a hundred degrees outside." Cora shook her head. "And what's this about firing another Santa."

"Yes, he was sending the kids all down to Farnsworth's for their big sale."

"He what?"

"Sent the kids to Farnsworth's" J.B. sat down behind the desk.

"He said it wasn't him, but I was standing right there and heard it."

"Well, what do you expect?" Cora said, as she sat down in a chair in front of the desk.

"You've been picking lower quality Santa's for years. Just to save a little money."

"Every penny counts." J.B. defended himself.

"And look what you got for your money."

"I know. I know. But most regular folks here in town won't work for me."

"If I wasn't your wife I wouldn't work for you either." Cora laughed. "You're the cheapest man in town. And everybody knows it."

"Now Cora," J.B. whined. "I'm not really that cheap. I pay you a good salary."

"Only because I won't let you get away with paying me less than I'm worth." Cora stood. "C'mon, let's go get some lunch. You're buying."

****

Bertha Humble was not happy. The Mayor's snub of her generous offer had caused her some embarrassment with the ladies of the *Women Hoping For Equality Now Society*. Everyone in the room had heard the conversation. Bertha made sure it was on the speakerphone at the Society's office. But she didn't expect the result to be what it was. As she put the phone back on the desk and punched the button to terminate the connection and silence the speaker her face reflected the growing anger. *"How dare he talk to me that way,"* she thought. *"And in front of all these women. The nerve."*

"Bertha," it was Eloise Simonet, President of the Society. "I'm afraid that didn't turn out too well, dear." Eloise said, with just a hint of sarcasm. She was not Bertha's friend, although they shared many things in common. Eloise, however, resented Bertha's desire to replace her as the leader of the Society. So she took every opportunity to create situations that usually turned out to be problems for Bertha. And it looked like this one was definitely one of those situations.

"Well, I'm sure the Mayor is just feeling the stress of his office today." Bertha tried to cover up her embarrassment but it was obvious that this whole invitation thing had backfired.

"Yes," Eloise agreed, rather too quickly. "I'm sure that must be the case. He's never turned down one of my invitations. Possibly I should have called, do you think?" Eloise was beginning to have fun with Bertha's discomfort.

"No, Eloise, it was my idea." Bertha could barely contain her anger at Eloise for being ridiculed this way.

"And, after all," she continued, through clenched teeth and a forced smile. "If I'm going to be the new President of the Society it was my place to invite him." Bertha knew just what to say to put Eloise in her place.

"Yes, Bertha," Eloise spoke through clenched teeth of her own, without the smile. She had been embarrassed when she spoke at the City Council meeting. That night it was Bertha's idea, and Bertha's words, and Eloise got the grief. She wouldn't forget. "But I think you might have handled the Mayor with a little more finesse. Berating him for being slow to answer the phone certainly set the tone for your conversation."

Bertha didn't like the way this was going.

"Yes, Bertha." One of the other ladies spoke up. "After all, he is the Mayor. And he deserves a little more respect than you gave him."

"Quite so," Eloise agreed. "As the leading candidate for my job..."

"Leading Candidate?" Bertha nearly choked. "I'm the only candidate. Because I'm the only one here who isn't afraid of you. And when I am the President of this Society things will change around here." Suddenly Bertha realized that she had said more than she should.

There was total quiet in the room. Each of the ladies present had just had their worst fears realized. If Bertha became the President things would certainly change, and not for the better. From the beginning W.H.E.N had been more of a Social Club than an activist organization. An excuse to get together, without their husbands, and enjoy each other's company. Meeting nights were spent drinking coffee and sharing the latest gossip around Newton's Mill. In fact, one of the ladies suggested that W.H.E.N really stood for Women Having an Enjoyable Night. Each of them began to think that electing Bertha to replace Eloise might not be such a good idea. It had been Bertha's idea to oppose the Nativity Scene because it wasn't politically correct. Many of the women had fond memories of the caroling when it stood in front of the old mill. It was, they felt, a pleasant tradition.

"I mean," Bertha began to stammer. "I mean that when I'm President we will be a more visible Society, with lot's of involvement in the community." But the damage was done. "You know, charity drives, fund raisers, and stuff like that."

Eloise looked at Bertha, shook her head and walked away. One by one the women turned and followed her until Bertha found herself alone.

****

"What'll it be, Mr. Mayor?"

"Morning, Charlie. I guess I'll have the chicken salad and a large ice tea."

"Comin' right up. Mr. Mayor." Charlie turned to take the order to the kitchen, stopped and turned back to the Mayor. "Isn't it a little early for lunch?"

"Yes, it is. But there's a Fire Drill scheduled for City Hall, so we decided to take and early lunch."

"Fire drill? There's only four of you working there."

"I know, how hard can it be?"

"Right, that's just what I was gonna say." Charlie answered as he walked away, shaking his head.

"One chicken salad, comin' right up."

Charlie's favorite saying was "comin' right up" and he used it for just about everything. Charley had owned the little restaurant down the street from City Hall for over twenty years. When he first opened it up he wanted to call it McDonalds, but finally settled on Charlie's Place. Something about not wanting to cause any confusion, even though his last name was MacDonald. And the Mayor had started having his lunches there when he had his law office just down the street, even before he was the Mayor. He just liked the easy atmosphere. The Food Court at J.B.'s was just too hectic. And G.D. didn't really like hectic.

"Excuse me, Mr. Mayor." It was someone G.D. didn't

recognize. "Mind if I join you?"

"I don't want to be rude," G. D. answered. "But if you want to talk about this Nativity Scene subject I'm afraid I'm not in the mood."

"No sir, Mr. Mayor. I'm from out of town and when I heard that fella call you Mr. Mayor I figured you would be just the person to talk to."

"Oh?"

"Yes, I'm sort of interested in the history of Newton's Mill. How it got its start, how long you've lived here. Things like that.

"Are you a reporter from a newspaper or magazine?" G. D. was still a little suspicious.

"No sir, just a curious traveler. I like small towns. Folks are almost always a lot more friendly and real in them than some of the big cities I've found. But if this isn't a good time I'll understand."

G.D. paused for a moment. *"It would be a relief to talk to someone about something other than this Nativity situation."* He thought. "Well, have a seat. Can I buy you a coffee or something?"

"No, actually I've already ordered and the owner, Charley I think you called him, said it would be common' right up." The stranger said, as he sat down.

"Yeah, that's Charlie's favorite saying. I don't think I caught your name."

"Oh, I'm sorry." The stranger offered his hand. "My name is Gabriel, but you can call me Gabe."

"Well, Gabriel, I mean Gabe, where should I start."

"The beginning is always good."

The Mayor laughed. "Right. Well, the town wasn't always called Newton's Mill. It was known as Bethlehem Township..." The Mayor paused in mid sentence.

"What is it?" Gabriel looked closely at the Mayor.

"Oh, nothing. I just hadn't thought of what the original name of the town was in a long time. Actually, the story goes that that was the reason Colonel Newton had the Nativity Scene created. Because the town was called Bethlehem Township back then."

"Bethlehem Township, eh?" Gabriel asked. "Anyway, go on."

G. D. continued. "Well, as I said, it was called Bethlehem Township until Colonel Rufus Newton built the mill. Then over the years folks just started referring to the town as Newton's Mill Town and pretty soon the name was shortened to Newton's Mill and the town was incorporated under that name."

"Here you are, fellas." It was Charley with their orders. "One chicken salad and an ice tea for the Mayor and a Charlie's special burger for the stranger, here."

"Gabriel" the tall man said. "The name is Gabriel, but you can just call me Gabe."

"Right you are, and a large soda for Gabe." Charlie set the orders down in front of the two men, paused to wipe his hands on his apron, then turned as a young couple entered and sat down in a booth near the window. "Enjoy." He said as he turned away.

"Do you mind if I bless the food?" Gabriel asked.

"Why, no. I was about to but go ahead." The Mayor said as he folded his hands on his lap and bowed his head.

"Father, we ask your blessing on this food, and this time of fellowship. May it strengthen our bodies for the work ahead?" Gabriel's voice was firm and easily heard by others in the restaurant. "And bless the Mayor in the awesome task he has of governing this community. Bless him with wisdom, understanding and strength. We ask it in the name of your Son, Jesus. Amen"

"Thank you, Gabriel." G.D. looked up as he spoke. "I appreciate the prayer. Especially the wisdom part."

As the two of them began to eat Gabriel asked the Mayor to continue with his story.

"Oh, right. Well, the town began to prosper when the Mill was up and running and folks began to come in to work at it. But it didn't really start to take off until folks realized just how cheap the land was around here and we started growing houses faster than food."

"I've seen that happen in other places, as well." Gabriel spoke between bites. "Did it change the town much?"

"Not at first. But then the folks from the big city to the East began to get involved in the community and that brought about changes. Some good, some not so good."

"Such as?"

"Well, we have a lot better school system than in the early days. We have four grade schools and two High Schools and another getting ready to be built over on the West end of town. Lots of business followed the population growth. And, of course, we have the big shopping mall downtown."

"You mean J.B. Nickels' place?'

"You know it?"

"Sort of. I applied for a job as a Santa Claus for the Christmas Season."

"Oh, really? And how did that go?'

"Not good. I guess J. B. was a little intimidated by my size and washed me out in the first cut." Gabriel laughed. "It's all for the best, though. I'm not sure I could have worked for a man like

Nickels."

"Not many can." G.D. agreed. "He gets most of his Santa's from the homeless shelter.'

"That's what I figured when I saw the candidates."

"And he pays them practically nothing."

"That's unfortunate. A man with his resources could be a real benefit to the city."

"If only he would recognize that. Anyway, to get on with the story. When the farmers began to sell out the Mill just gradually went to nothing and finally shut down. It was a pretty sad day for the folks who had lived here all their lives. Most of them had worked in the Mill at one time or another. And during the war the Newton family gave jobs to a lot of the women folk while their men were away."

"Sounds like they were real community minded."

"They were. Lots of folks called them angels for all they did."

"They might have been, Mr. Mayor." Gabriel mused. "They might have been."

****

"Well, that looks like that's everything on the list." Hebert mumbled to himself as he stood in the produce aisle scanning the

list Bertha had left him. *"There's enough food here for a hundred people. At least it looks that way."* Hebert made his way to the checkout stand, saying hello and nodding to folks he recognized. Some offered a greeting, others shook his hand and some even took him to task for voting against the Nativity scene. But it was all done good-naturedly. Most folks in town who knew Hebert and Bertha recognized the situation with them and did their best to be pleasant to Hebert. Most of them were not as considerate of Bertha. Which only made things worse for Hebert.

"Well, say there, Councilman Humble." It was Galena Bauxite, part owner of the Shopping Bag market, and a long time admirer of Hebert. She had had a crush on him since grade school and was pretty broken up when Bertha snared him. "Looks like you have enough food here for an army. Havin' company?"

"Good morning Galena." Hebert said with a halfhearted smile as he began loading items on the conveyor belt. "Bertha is having a dinner party for some of the ladies from W.H.E.N. tonight."

"Looks like there's enough food here for half the town." Galena laughed.

"Yes, well, you know Bertha likes to make a big impression." Hebert finished unloading his cart, paid for the items and started to leave.

"Hebert," Galena was serious. "Is everything alright with you and Bertha? You just don't look happy."

"Indigestion." Hebert said, as he walked away.

"Yeah, right. Indigestion." Galena thought as she turned to the next customer in line.

Hebert made his way across the parking lot to his car, loaded the bags in the trunk and took the cart back to the area set aside for them. He always put things back when he was through with them.

Climbing into his car he sat for a moment before starting it. *"I guess it shows."* He thought. *"How can it not. I'm not happy. And it's my own fault. I should stand up to Bertha."* Shaking his head he started the car and pulled out of the parking lot. Hebert drove home, unloaded the items from the car and put them in their places. Bertha had a plan for the kitchen. "A place for everything." She always told him. And it was not in his best interests to ever put something where it didn't belong. He folded up the bags and put them in the drawer, looked around the kitchen for a moment and then made his way back to the car.

It was about a fifteen-minute trip to the parking lot at J.B. Nickels and, after parking the car, he made the long walk to the entrance. Hebert always parked at the farthest point in the lot so as not to anger J.B. who monitored where the employees and storeowners parked and was known to leave nasty notes under the wipers on their cars.

Katie Brown looked up from her desk as Hebert entered the store. "Good Morning, Mr. H." She called cheerfully. She was always glad to see him and always called him Mr. H. affectionately. He had been, for many years, like a father to her. "Busy morning?'

"Busy enough, Katie. Bertha is having a bunch of people from that..." Hebert paused, searching for a word, then decided better of it. "...Organization she belongs to over for dinner. And I just finished the shopping."

"Well, it's been pretty quiet around here, so far." Katie got up from her desk and walked to where Hebert stood.

"Have you had your lunch, yet?" He asked.

"No, I was waiting for you so you could sit in while I went."

"Good girl. I'm here now so why don't you head over and get something to eat?"

"Okay. Can I get you anything?"

Hebert reached into his pocket a pulled out a handful of bills. "Bring me back a deli sandwich from that underground sandwich shop and a large soda."

"You got it, Mr. H. See you in a bit." Katie left the store.

Hebert sat down behind his desk just as the phone rang.

"Hello"

"Hebert!" It was Bertha, and she was not happy. The turn of events at the meeting caused her to need to lash out at something, or someone. And Hebert was it.

"Yes, dear. What is it?"

"Did you finish all the chores I had for you before you went down to that good for nothing bookstore of yours?" She nearly shouted. "And the shopping? Did you do the shopping?"

"Yes dear. It's all done and put away just the way you like it." Hebert couldn't help the little note of sarcasm that crept into his voice.

Bertha was quick to pick up on it. "Don't you get snippy with me, Hebert Humble. Just remember whose money it is that you used to start up that loser bookstore of yours."

Hebert sat silently.

"Hebert, are you there?" Bertha didn't like it when he didn't answer her.

"Yes, dear. I'm still here."

"It looks like there will only be eleven people at our dinner tonight."

"Oh?"

"Yes, the Mayor declined my invitation."

"Way to go." Hebert mumbled to himself. Pleased at the Mayor's refusal to subject himself to Bertha's attacks.

"What did you say?" Bertha shouted.

"I said I think it might snow."

"Well, if it starts you better get home in plenty of time to fix dinner."

"Me?"

"Yes, you. You don't expect me to do it?" Bertha was beginning to enjoy this. "I can't be home slaving over a hot stove with guests coming. You will just have to do it." And with that she slammed down the phone, causing Hebert to jump.

"Wonderful." He thought. *"Just wonderful. With all the things I have to do here now I have to get this ridiculous dinner party ready."*

Hebert was still deep in thought when Katie returned with their lunch. "Hey. Mr. H. You don't look so good. What's up?"

"Indigestion." Hebert answered.

"Indigestion named Bertha?" Katie asked. She had seen the symptoms before.

"Yes. Now she wants me to prepare this dinner for her group

tonight." Hebert opened his sandwich. "So I'll have to leave early."

"Say, Mr. H. I'm a pretty good cook." Katie offered between bites of her sandwich. "Want some help?"

"That's nice of you to offer but someone needs to watch the store. I'll just finish my sandwich and head back home. There's a lot to be done."

"Okay, Mr. H, whatever you say.

Katie and Hebert finished their lunch in silence.

****

Jane, Jim, Paul and Sam found a table near the window of the Pizza restaurant in the Food Court.

"So" Paul asked. "What kind of Pizzas do we want? And don't say peanut butter. That's gross."

The others laughed.

"Yeah, did you see the look on the Mayor's face when you mentioned it?" Sam said.

"Oh, man, I sure did. I thought he was gonna barf right there."

"Alright, that's enough you two." Jane always had to referee when the four of them got together for lunch, or sometimes for coffee after work. "I think I want the vegetarian."

"There you go, always trying to make us think you're some kind of wholesome food addict." Paul chided. "When what you really want is the super deluxe, four kinds of meat and four kinds of cheese with onions, peppers and garlic, heart attack in a pan, pizza."

"Very funny." Jane couldn't help herself and laughed as hard as the rest of them. "I'll have whatever the rest of you want."

"Good." Jim got up from the table and headed for the counter to order. "I'll choose."

"Oh oh. I think we're in trouble."

"I just hope he doesn't order that garlic chicken one. I don't want to spend the rest of my afternoon cooped up in that tiny office with a bunch of people with garlic on their breath." Sam joked.

"What are you talkin' about, Sam." Jane turned to him. "You work all over the building."

"Right, and it's a small building."

Jim walked back to the table. "You guys are safe. I ordered the Hawaiian pizza and a large pitcher of beer."

"BEER?" The other three shouted.

"Yeah, root."

"Look over there." Paul interrupted. "Looks like Katie's getting lunch for her and Hebert." Paul really liked Katie, and it was pretty obvious she felt the same way. They had been friends since Kindergarten, as had many of the folks who went to Rufus Newton Grade School back when it was the only school in town. It was pretty much taken for granted that they would get married as soon as Paul got up enough nerve to ask her.

Katie caught sight of the four of them through the window, got a big smile and waved as she went by.

"Well, I reckon that big smile was for you, Paul" Sam said. "She sure is a pretty young lady."

"Yeah, Paul." Jayne asked. "When are you gonna pop the big question?"

"C'mon you guys." Jim spoke up. "Paul's just a little shy. He can't help it if every time he gets close to her he gets so tongue-tied he can't talk."

"I do not."

"That isn't what she told me." Jayne looked at Paul. "She says that when the two of you are together you just sit and look at her with this funny look on your face."

"I do not."

"I saw the two of them walking hand in hand the other day. He couldn't take his eyes off of her. Nearly ran into a telephone pole."

Sam joined in.

"I did not."

"Would have, too, if she hadn't pulled you aside at the last second."

"She did not."

"Hey, Jim." The clerk at the counter called out. "Your Pizza's ready. Peanut butter, just like you ordered."

"Aaagh!" The others groaned.

"Just joking. Come and get it."

Jim got up from the table and went to pick up the pizza. Katie, on her way back from the underground sandwich shop stuck her head in the door.

"Hey, you guys, what are you doing here so early? It isn't even noon yet."

"Hi, Katie." Jayne smiled. "Fire chief wanted to have a fire drill at City Hall so the Mayor and all of us evacuated the building ahead of it."

"A fire drill?"

"Yep"

"Only five of you work there, right?"

"Right."

"So how hard can it be?"

"That's exactly what we said. Gettin' lunch for you and Hebert?"

"Right. Bertha had him running errands all morning so I offered to pick us up something because he looked so exhausted when he came in."

Paul sat quietly through the conversation, just staring at Katie.

"Hi, Paul." Katie caught him staring at her. "Are we still on for Saturday night?"

"Ugh, Saturday night?'

"You know, the movies?"

Oh, right, the movies. Sure. I'll pick you up at the usual time." Paul's face turned crimson.

"Good. See you guys. Gotta get these sandwiches to Mr. H. before he expires." And with that she hurried off to the bookstore.

"Well, you sure handled that well." Sam smiled at Paul. "You are a real Casanova, you are."

Jim returned and put the steaming hot pizza in the center of the table, handed small plates and napkins to everyone and they began to eat.

****

"Well, Gabriel," The mayor said. "That's pretty much the whole story of Newton's Mill."

They had been talking and eating for nearly an hour. Gabriel was a good listener and G.D. was happy to be discussing something other than the Nativity Scene controversy. "Hope it didn't bore you."

"No, actually it was quite interesting. I love small towns, and their history."

"Ah, yes, but Newton's Mill isn't much of a small town anymore."

"But it still has lots of small town ways. Like the diner here. And many of the folks are more than friendly, even to a stranger."

"Well, I'm glad you think so. Are you planning on being in town for awhile?"

"Well," Gabriel said softly. "I have some business that will keep me here a few more days. In fact, I think I would like to stick around for the City Council Meeting, next Tuesday."

"Here it comes," Thought G.D. *"I was hoping it wouldn't get around to this."*

"The Council Meeting?" He asked aloud.

"Yes, this whole scenario surrounding the Nativity Scene is very interesting. And historical."

"Historical?"

"Yes," Gabriel said as he stood up and dropped some change on the table for a tip. "The Nativity has been pretty controversial for a couple thousand years. See you again, Mr. Mayor."

G.D. watched him as he paid his check and made his way out of the diner. *"I wonder what he meant by that?"* He thought. *"Oh well, better be getting back to City Hall. Smokey should have finished his fire drill by now."* He dropped a bill on the table for Charley's good service, paid his check, and left.

****

Hebert was in the midst of preparing the baked potatoes for the oven when the doorbell rang. *"Who could that be?"* He thought. *"Not some door to door salesman I hope."* Removing his apron he laid it across the back of a chair and made his way to the front door. *"I really don't have time for interruptions."*

Hebert opened the door to find a smiling Katie standing there. "Hi, Mr. H." She said as she pushed past him. "Which way is the kitchen?"

"Katie? What are you doing here?"

"I'm here to help you get this gourmet meal prepared." She

laughed. "Besides, the store was quiet and so I figured you could use some help. What's on the menu?"

Hebert stood, speechless.

"Come on, Mr. H. We don't have much time. Which way is the kitchen and what's on the menu?"

"Uh, well, right this way." Hebert recovered his voice and led the way to the kitchen. "Bertha wants pork roast with baked potatoes, corn on the cob and apple pie for desert."

"Okay, I'll do the apple pie and the corn, you handle the pot roast." And Katie went right to work.

They worked in silence except for Katie asking questions about where certain things were.

Turned out that they were a pretty good team and the dinner was ready in no time.

"Katie," Hebert said, as she removed the pie from the oven. "That looks really delicious."

"It's my Mom's recipe. She's taught me how to cook since I was a little girl. I love it, and apple pie is my specialty."

"Well, I guess she taught you well."

"Mr. H., I'm glad I was able to help. Now I better get home before my Mom wonders where I am."

"Katie, I can't thank you enough for all your help. Your Mom and Dad are lucky to have you."

"Oh, it's just my Mom and I. My Dad went home about four years ago."

"Went home?"

"Yes, to be with The Lord." Katie said softly. "He had cancer pretty bad."

"I'm sorry to hear that. I never knew." Hebert and Katie's Dad had been friends in school but after his marriage to Bertha they lost touch. It was a shock to hear that he had died.

"It's okay, Mr. H. He's in a lot better place now. See you tomorrow at the store." Katie draped her apron over a chair. "I can find my way out." And she left.

Hebert picked up Katie's apron, took off his own and tossed them in the laundry hamper. He went into the dining room and began to set the table.

"Went home." He said aloud. "That's interesting. I never thought of it that way. Makes it seem easier, somehow." He continued setting the table, folded the napkins just the way Bertha liked them, and then went into the kitchen to check on the food. Everything was ready for tonight. *"I hope it turns out well for Bertha."* He thought. In spite of how she treated him he cared for her. But he knew she only tolerated him. *"If this turns out well for* her, maybe she won't be so angry all the time." He thought. *"That would be nice."*

****

Jayne, Jim, and Paul were already at work in the office when G.D arrived.

"Well, public servants," G.D. laughed. "I see you are all back at your desks, deserving of the taxpayer's money." "Right you are, Mr. Mayor." Paul said. "But I think you've been spending too much time with Councilman Archibald. You're starting to sound like him."

"Oh, I hope not. Did Smokey get his Fire Drill all wrapped up?"

"I guess so," Jayne answered. "City Hall was pretty much deserted when we got back."

"Where did you guys go for lunch? Some exotic restaurant?"

"Real exotic. We went to the pizza parlor." Jim answered. "And Paul had a chance to see his favorite bookstore clerk."

"Come on, Jim. Give it a rest." Paul shot back.

"Favorite bookstore clerk, eh?" G.D. smiled. "That wouldn't be Katie Black, now would it?"

"The very same." Jayne said.

"Well, I don't blame you a bit, Paul. She's a sweet girl and I've known her folks forever. It was pretty tough on her when her Dad died a while back. He was a great guy. You could do worse."

"Thanks, Mr. Mayor." Paul appreciated the Mayor's input. "But these guys just won't leave me alone about her. Makes me embarrassed."

"You shouldn't be. I'm sure they just do it out of jealousy. You two planning on tying the knot any time soon?"

"Aw, come on, Mr. Mayor, not you, too."

"Just joking, Paul. Just Joking."

"Mr. Mayor, I hate to change the subject but I put some papers on your desk that really need to be signed today." Jayne interrupted. "And as for Paul popping the question to Katie. I'm not sure he's brave enough to ask her."

"I am, too." Paul almost shouted. "I mean I'm waiting for the right time. No, what I mean is..."

"That's okay, Paul. We understand." Jim said, going over and putting his hand on Paul's shoulder. "She is so pretty she just takes your breath away."

"And his mind, too." Jayne laughed.

Paul just rolled his eyes and went back to his paperwork. "You guys are somethin' else."

G.D. went into his office, sat down at the desk and busied himself with the papers that Jayne had left for him until it was time to head home.

****

It was 6:30 at the Humble household and things were not good. So far no one had bothered to show up for Bertha's dinner. In fact, no one had even called. Hebert sat at the kitchen table with Bertha, who was unusually quiet.

"Are you sure they had the time right?" Hebert asked.

"Yes, I'm sure." Bertha almost yelled. "I gave everyone an engraved invitation. Except for the Mayor."   "Well, we know he isn't coming." Hebert mumbled.

"What?" Bertha growled.

"I said we know the Mayor isn't coming."

"Is that supposed to be funny?"

"No, just a statement."

"Well, keep your statements to yourself."

The two of them sat in silence for a while longer and then Hebert got up and turned off the oven where the food was staying warm.

"Bertha, I don't think anyone is coming."

Bertha just sat and glared at him.

"Did something happen at the meeting today?"

"No, nothing happened at the meeting." Bertha wasn't about to let Hebert know how embarrassed she was and how the group snubbed her after her little outburst.

"Well, there must be some reason why no one is showing up for your dinner."

"They're not showing up because they're all just a bunch of women who like to sit around and talk and play cards and eat. Not one of them is interested in making a difference."

"So, something did happen at the meeting?"

"Oh, it's none of your business. I'm going up to bed."

"What shall I do with all this food?"

"I don't care." Bertha said, as she stormed out of the kitchen. "Eat it yourself."   Hebert stood quietly in the middle of the kitchen as he watched Bertha go. *"That's a lot of food."* He thought. *"It would take us a week to eat it all as leftovers."*

He began to gather containers from the cabinets and put the food into them. He got a box from the basement and arranged the containers in it, put a towel over it, and got his jacket from the hall closet.

"Bertha," He called up the stairs. "I'm going out for a few minutes."

No answer.

"Oh well," He thought. *"She won't miss me."*

Hebert gathered up the box, went to his car and put it in the trunk. He got into the car, started it and pulled out of the driveway.

"The folks at the homeless shelter are gonna eat good, tonight." He laughed.

****

Thursday

"Mornin', G.D." Helen was at the stove and the smell of bacon frying filled the room. "How did you sleep?"

"Like a baby," The Mayor replied.

"Really?"

"Yeah, I kept waking up all night and crying."

"What?"

"Just joking. I guess I slept pretty good, considering."

"Considering?'

"Considering I can't get this Nativity stuff off my mind. I guess I never thought something so simple as a yes or no vote could have so much importance."

"You suppose folks are overreacting?"

"I don't know. Some of them seem to be. And it's both sides of the argument. Yesterday a bunch of kids cornered me in the park and wanted to know what I was gonna do about Christmas."

"And?"

"And no matter how I tried I couldn't convince them that this vote wasn't gonna cancel Christmas."

G.D. went to the stove and poured himself a cup of coffee from the

percolator. Helen preferred brewing her coffee the same way her mom had done for years. No fancy drip coffee for her. She even ground the beans fresh, every morning. "Best cup of coffee in town." G.D. always said.

"Well, you might have saved yourself all this grief if you had just voted at the Council meeting."

"That's just it. I'm not sure which way I would have voted."

"You're not sure?" Helen came over to the table and set a plate of bacon and eggs in front of G.D. "How else would you have voted but yes?"

"I know that seems to be the easy answer. But is it the right answer?"

"Why wouldn't it be?"

"Helen, Newton's Mill isn't what it used to be. It's grown and gotten more like a big city. And I have to make a decision that's right for the whole community."

"And voting yes wouldn't be right for the whole community?"

"Not for the folks that don't want that Nativity Scene on government property."

"G.D., are you making this into a big deal?"

"What do you mean am I making this into a big deal?"

"Do you remember last year when the subject of water meters came up before the council?"

"Oh boy, do I. That was some meeting."

"If I remember correctly it went on for hours."

"It was after midnight before I could call for a vote."

"And what happened when you called for a vote?"

G.D. sat quietly for a minute, remembering the arguments both for and against the water meters. With the growth of the town it was getting harder and harder to cover the cost of supplying water and meters seemed to be the only answer.

"Well, the council was deadlocked at two for and two against."

"And?"

"And I had to cast the tie breaking vote."

"You voted for the meters."

"Yes."

"Did the world come to and end?"

"No, in fact, after a few weeks of turmoil folks seemed to accept the meters as a necessary evil and things quieted down."

"Right, and the same thing will probably happen with this Nativity flap, as well."

"I'm not so sure, Helen."

"Why not?"

"Well, I've never had to vote for or against God before."

****

Hebert was pouring himself a cup of coffee when Bertha swept into the room. Without a word she sat down at the table waiting for

Hebert to bring her a cup of coffee. He took the one he had just poured over to her and got another cup from the cupboard. He noticed that Bertha didn't look so good.

"What's the matter, dear?" He asked. "You look like something's bothering you."

Bertha sat staring at her coffee cup for a moment and then looked up. "What did you do with the left over food from that disaster last night?"

"Well," Hebert could see that trouble was brewing. "I figured we could never eat all of that food ourselves, so I boxed it up and took it to the homeless shelter."

"THE HOMELESS SHELTER?" Bertha erupted. "You took all that expensive food to the homeless shelter? What in the world ever prompted you to give our food to that bunch of losers down there?"

"They're not losers, Bertha. Just people who are down on their luck right now."

"Down on their luck, eh? Bertha snorted. "Lazy good for nothing losers that's what they are. Don't you ever throw our food away like that again."

"Yes, dear." Hebert knew there was no sense in arguing with her. He never won. "What is your day like, today?" He asked, trying to change the subject.

Bertha didn't answer. It was none of Hebert's business what she did today. After last night's disaster she decided to take a trip to the city to do some shopping. Maybe have lunch in a fancy restaurant, befitting her station. Anything to get away from the narrow minded little people of Newton's Mill. *"I don't belong in such a backward town as this."* she thought. *"My ideas are too big for anyone here."* And an idea began to form in her mind.

"I guess I'll spend the day at the store." Hebert tried to get the conversation on to something less stressful. "Got a new shipment of books in yesterday that have to be..."

"Oh, who cares?" Bertha interrupted. "Who cares about that grimy little book store of yours? It's just like you, little and worthless. I don't know why I ever married you." And with that Bertha got up from the table and stormed out of the house. And the idea grew even more in her mind.

Hebert sat quietly for a moment, then got up walked to the kitchen window, just in time to see Bertha roaring out of the driveway and down the street. He poured himself another cup of coffee and sat back down at the table. *"I guess I don't know why she married me, either."* He thought. *"Must be my animal magnetism."* And he laughed at his own joke.

****

Katie Black missed her dad. Even after four years she still missed him a lot. Those last few years, as he was suffering from cancer, were really tough on her and her Mom and it was a blessing when he finally went home. But she still missed him.

"I guess that's why I like Mr. H. so much," She told her Mom. "He's a lot like Dad."

They were sitting at the breakfast table and Katie had been telling her Mom about helping Hebert prepare the dinner last night.

"I sure hope Mrs. H. appreciated all the work we did."

"I've known Bertha Humble since we were in the first grade together," Her Mom said. "I would bet you anything she didn't. I've never known her to appreciate anything anyone did for her.

"Mr. H. is such a nice man. How did he ever wind up with her?" "He almost didn't have a choice. She could see he was a gentle soul that she could ride herd on pretty good and so she just decided that they were gonna get married, and they did."

"Did you know Mr. H. before they got married?"

Katie's Mom laughed. "I sure did. Hebert and I were best friends until Bertha set her sights on him. After that he couldn't be friends with anybody but Bertha."

"That's pretty sad."

"Well, Hebert has a good heart. Too good in some ways. In all the years I've known him I've never heard him talk bad about anybody. And, before Bertha, he was always helping somebody or other, cutting old Mrs. Anderson's yard, helping out at the homeless shelter, stuff like that."

"Before Bertha?"

"After Bertha got her hooks into him he wasn't allowed to do things like that for the 'little people'."

"Little people?"

"Yes, anyone that Bertha figured was beneath her. And that was most near everybody. I don't think Hebert's had a day for himself since."

"Well, I better head for the store." Katie said, getting up from the table and taking her breakfast dishes to the sink. "We got a big shipment of books in yesterday and, since I closed the store early to go help Mr. H., I haven't had a chance to work on them. See you later, Mom." Katie kissed her mom on the cheek and headed out the door.

"So long, Honey. Drive carefully." Her Mom called after her.

****

J. B. Nickels stopped off at the Happy Gourmet Coffee Shoppe each morning before going to the store. He always ordered the same thing. A large coffee with plenty of cream and sugar, he liked it sweet, and a blueberry muffin. Then he sat in one of the small booths near the front of the shop so he could watch the workers and early shoppers as they made their way through the Mall.

"There goes Katie Black on her way to Hebert's little book store." He thought. *"I wonder how they're doing? Might be a chance to raise their rent if business has been good. I don't know how he stays open, though. Probably wouldn't if it wasn't for Bertha's money."*

Everyone in town knew that Bertha had been the financing behind the bookstore. She never missed a chance to let folks know that she put up the money for the store to give Hebert something to do with his time. "And keep him out of my hair." She always joked.

"Excuse me, Mr. Nickels," It was the tall man from the Santa Claus interviews. J.B. hadn't noticed him come into the shop. "Might I join you?"

"Eh?" J.B. was not ready for that.

"I just wanted to take a minute and apologize for my attitude at the interviews yesterday."

"Won't do you any good." J.B. was back in control of himself. "I've hired all the Santas I need."

The tall man laughed. "Oh, that's okay, I'm not looking for a job. Actually, I have one."

"That's good. You're too tall for a Santa anyway." J.B. didn't want to appear too friendly but somehow he found he liked this tall stranger, in spite of what happened at the interview. "And I accept your apology."

"Great." The tall man sat down across from J.B. and began to sip his coffee. "How's the muffin?" He asked.

J.B. wasn't really in the mood for small talk. "It's good, as always."

"I wanted to take a minute and get your feelings about this Nativity Scene situation."

"My feelings should be obvious since I voted against it at the council meeting Tuesday night."

"I know, I was there."

"You were?" J.B. didn't recall seeing him.

"Yes, at the back of the room, just inside the door."

Now J. B. was sure he hadn't seen him there. "That's strange. I usually pay close attention to attendees at the council meetings. Customers, you know. And I don't remember you."

"Well, sometimes, even as tall as I am, I don't stand out in a crowd."

"Maybe so." J.B. still was sure he hadn't seen him there. "You're new to our town, aren't you?"

"Yes, just got in Tuesday afternoon." The tall man took another sip of his coffee. "This is very good coffee."

"So what made you decide to attend the Council meeting?"

"I figured it was the best place to find out what are the important issues, and who are the important people, in the town."

"And?"

"Well, I was a little surprised by all the concern about the Nativity Scene. Maybe you could tell me why you voted against it?"

"Why are you so interested in this?"

"Well, the Nativity scene just sort of seems like a very important part of Christmas. Don't you agree?"

"The important part of Christmas for me is sales, sales, sales. And the Nativity Scene doesn't generate business." J.B. answered.

"Which doesn't generate sales, sales, sales, right?"

"Right. Christmas is about buying stuff, and giving gifts and spending money."

"You have part of that right."

"Part?"

"Yes, the part about giving gifts."

"Giving gifts?"

"Yes, actually the Nativity Scene is about a gift. For everyone. Think about that." And the tall man stood up to leave. "Remember, J. B. Nickels, you can't take it with you." He said as he walked away.

"I wonder what he meant by that." J.B. thought.

****

The Reverend Artemis Brown sat at the desk in his study staring at the screen on his desktop computer. He always liked to start work on his Sunday sermon on Thursday to give himself plenty of time to prepare. But, somehow or other, this morning was different.

"Can't seem to get my thoughts together." He spoke out loud. "Maybe I need another cup of coffee." He stood up from the desk and made his way to the kitchen. The Brown home was small in comparison to some of the newer homes being built near him. But Artemis loved this old house. It had belonged to his family for many years. His dad had built it a few years after going to work at the Mill and he had many fond memories of growing up here.

When he went away to college, and then to the professional football team on the West Coast, he always enjoyed coming home for visits. And when his mother passed away they held the reception after the funeral in the large yard that surrounded the house. Nearly everyone in town attended. It was the first time Artemis had been home in several years and he enjoyed being back.

Playing professional football was fun for Artemis but deep in his heart he wanted to be a man of God. So, when his contract was up he walked away from the fame and the money and returned to college for his divinity degree. It was when he came back to Newton's Mill for his father's funeral that he decided to stay in the little house they had loved, and start his church.

"Any more coffee in that pot, honey." He said to his wife. "Need to jump start my brain."

"Artemis Brown, you've already had three cups this mornin', and that's two over your limit." His wife laughed.

Artemis had met Samantha Davis at college and they had been married just after graduation. He had worried about bringing her back to Newton's Mill because she was a big city girl who enjoyed the excitement of the city. To his surprise she accepted the change and settled in to the little house quickly, adding little touches here and there to make it their home. He always thanked God for bringing Samantha into his life.

"Well, I have to do somethin' to get my brain workin', 'cause my sermon for Sunday just ain't comin' along."

"Well, then, Mr. Artemis Brown, ex-professional football player, why don't you just get your hat and your jacket and take a walk."

"Aw, Sam, I would much rather have a cup of coffee and sit here and look at you."

"Yeah, right. Here's your jacket. Walk down to the park, maybe an angel will come help you with your sermon."

"But, I got an angel right here." He said. putting his arms around her in a big bear hug. "Don't need to go to the park."

"Mmmf nnn." Samantha said from inside the bear hug.

"What did you say?"

Pulling away from him she said, "I said let go of me I got work to do. Now get on out of here."

"Okay," He said, pulling on his jacket. "I'm goin', I'm goin'." And he went out the door.

****

"Good morning, Jayne." The Mayor said as he entered the office. "Here all by yourself?"

"Yes, Jim and Paul walked over to Humble's book store to

check on the new shipment of books that came in yesterday."

"I didn't know they were so interested in books."

"They're not. But Paul is sure interested in Katie. So Jim went along just to torment him, I think. They said they would be back in a bit."

"Poor Paul. It's a good thing he has such an even temper or all that teasing would get him mad." The Mayor said.

"Not Paul. The only thing I've ever seen him get excited about works at Humble's Book Store."

"Katie?"

"Katie."

"Well, since it's just you and me I need to talk to you a bit."

"What's up, Mr. Mayor?"

"I sort of need to get your feelings about this whole Nativity Scene thing."

"My feelings?"

"Yes, I don't mind telling you that it has got me in a quandary. I've got to vote one way or the other next Tuesday night and so I need some input from folks without an ax to grind or an agenda to push."

"Jayne sat for a moment, gathering her thoughts. "Well," she finally spoke. "I kind of like the Nativity Scene. It just sort of seems like it feels more like Christmas when I see it. You know I'm active in Pastor Brown's Church, even sing in the choir?"

"I know, Jayne, I enjoy seeing you up there every Sunday morning."

"Well, the Nativity Scene going up sort of kicks off the Christmas season for me. We start rehearsing the music we will sing for Christmas and each morning, as I come to work, I see it out there in front of City Hall and it just seems right."

"It's been around for awhile." The mayor smiled.

"Longer than me."

"Longer than me, too. But when I was a kid, and the town was a lot smaller, we used to gather around it, all the townsfolk, and sing Christmas Carols. That was before the Mill closed and we moved it here to City Hall."

"You know, that would be a nice tradition to bring back."

"I think, maybe, the town is too big for that now. Too many people."

"I don't know. Seems like there isn't much Christmas spirit anymore. Might be just the thing to get it started again."

"So, what you're saying is that if it were you, you would

vote...?"

"I'd vote for it. Just because we're a big town now doesn't mean we can't keep our small town traditions." Jayne answered. "But. that's just me. I know you have to think about all the other folks in town and how they feel. But, for me, I like the Nativity Scene being on the front lawn of City Hall. I like seeing it after it snows, and lit up at night. To me, it's just says Christmas."

****

"This little town isn't big enough for me." Bertha thought as she sped through town and on to the throughway towards the East. *"My ideas are too important, I'm too important, to be wasted in this little backwoods Mill town.*

And the idea grew bigger in her mind.

****

Ira Freethinker and Phil Faithless sat together at a small table in the back of the Underground Sandwich Shop discussing their next course of action in the fight against the Nativity Scene. It wasn't going too good.

"Your argument Tuesday night didn't get much support, John." Phil spoke softly. The two of them always spoke in near whispers because they were afraid someone would overhear them.

"It's Ira, Phil, Ira."

"Oh, right, I keep forgetting. Ira, your argument Tuesday..."

"I heard you the first time, Phil." Ira interrupted.

"Oh, sorry."

"It's obvious the people in this town have no concept of the bigger picture here."

"Right, Ira." Phil hesitated a moment, as if trying to get his thoughts together. "What picture?"

Ira was still trying to decide if joining up with Phil had been a good idea. He just didn't seem passionately committed to the AAA concept.

"The wasting of taxpayers money to display this Nativity Scene on Government property. As Atheists we must always be at the forefront of the fight against religion."

"Amen," Phil said, without thinking.

"Will you stop that?" Ira snarled. "That word does not belong in any of our conversations."

"Gee, Ira, I'm sorry. I just keep forgetting." Phil apologized. "What's our next move?"

"We have to make people understand that the whole Nativity story is just a fairy tale."

"It is?"

"Of course it is. How could anyone believe that whole 'virgin birth' myth? If there is no God, then the whole thing is just a fairy tale. And we believe there is no God."

"Do we? I mean, we do." Now, Phil still wasn't too sure about all this "no God" stuff. He had been raised in Pastor Brown's church and still remembered the Christmas story. Phil didn't make friends easily and when he got hooked up with Ira while they were away at college he joined the AAA when Ira did. It was then that they changed their names from John and Richard to Ira and Phil. Phil's Mom still called him Richard, though.

But with Ira it was different. He was raised in a home where the name of God was used as a curse, if it was ever used at all, and his Mom and Dad laughed at anything religious. "Never been in a church, never gonna be." His Dad always said. So it was easy for him to believe there was no God, and when he had the opportunity to be the local representative of the AAA in Newton's Mill he jumped at the chance to "be somebody". But he had to admit it wasn't easy being an Atheist in Newton's Mill. Every time he saw Pastor Brown he would cross the street to avoid him. The one conversation he had with the ex-footballer turned Pastor, nearly scared him to death. Not believing in God was one thing, facing Pastor Brown was something else entirely.

"If that Nativity Scene goes up we've failed." Ira said. "And the Society doesn't like failure. So we have to convince folks that it's the wrong thing to do."

"So, how do we do that?"

"I have some money from the Society to help in this fight and I'm going down to the Newton Mill Press and take out a full page ad denouncing this whole Nativity Scene and the idea behind it."

"The idea behind it? What idea behind it?"

"The idea of God, Phil." Ira snarled through clenched teeth. "The idea that there is a God, and that He has relevance in today's world. Honestly, Phil, I sometimes think you aren't totally committed to our cause."

"Excuse me." It was the tall fellow, Gabriel. Ira and Phil looked up, way up, since Gabriel towered over their table like an avenging angel. That is, if Ira and Phil believed there were really angels. "I couldn't help but overhear your conversation. So you don't believe in God?"

"That's right," Ira said, standing up. "I don't," he said, sitting down when he saw that Gabriel was a full head and shoulders taller then he was. "I never have."

"How about you, Phil?" Gabriel looked into Phil's eyes.
"How did he know my name?" Phil thought. "Uh, well, yeah.

Me too. I don't believe in him, too. I think."

"But you used to, didn't you?" Gabriel asked.

"Say, listen," Ira interrupted. "This is a private conversation. Nobody asked you to get involved."

"Yeah," Phil said. "Nobody asked you." He didn't really want to continue talking with this tall stranger.

"Well, I just wanted to let you both know that there is a God, and He knows both your names, and He sees what you are doing. And the Nativity Scene isn't the worst of your problems." And Gabriel turned and walked away.

"What do you suppose he meant by that?" Phil asked.

****

Hebert parked his car at the back of the lot, as he usually did, and began the long walk to the Mall. *"This parking lot seems to get bigger everyday."* He thought. *"But the exercise is good for me, I guess."*

"Councilman Humble." The tall man spoke. "Might I walk a while with you?"

Hebert didn't see the tall man until he was right by his side. In fact, he almost seemed to come from nowhere. But then, Hebert was deep in thought so he must have just not noticed him.

"Excuse me," Hebert answered. "I don't believe I know you."

"The name's Gabriel. But, you can call me Gabe, if you like." The tall man said, offering Hebert his hand. "Just wanted to take a minute to tell you that it was a nice thing you did last night."

"Last night?"

"Yes, taking that food to the homeless shelter was very kind of you."

"Oh, that. Well, Bertha and I would have never been able to eat it all ourselves. And I knew those folks at the shelter would appreciate it."

"And they did." Gabriel said, as he fell in step beside Hebert. "They appreciate everything you do for them."

"What do you mean?"

"I guess not too many folks around here know just how much you support the center."

"Well, I have a lot, and they don't have much."

"But you get a lot of resistance from your wife, don't you?"

Hebert couldn't understand how this stranger knew so much about him. "Well, yes, Bertha isn't big on helping out those less fortunate than us."

"Well, I just want to let you know that your generosity plays an important part in keeping the center open."

"Thank you. That's nice to know. Are you new here in Newton's Mill? I don't think I've seen you before."

"Well, Councilman, Newton's Mill is getting bigger. I guess it would be hard to know everyone in town anymore."

"That's for sure. Are you new in town?"

"Yes, I got in on Tuesday. In fact, I was at the City Council Meeting that night."

"Oh, then you saw the controversy over the Nativity Scene."

"Yes, I did. I was quite surprised."

"Because of the resistance to placing it on the Courthouse lawn?"

"Actually, no. What surprised me was that you voted against it."

"Oh?"

"Yes, I don't think you really wanted to do that."

Hebert was beginning to wonder just who this tall fellow was. "Ah, yes, well, Bertha was dead set against it and she pretty much influences everything that I do, unfortunately."

"I know. That was the impression that I got. It's pretty much been that way hasn't it?"

"Sad to say." Hebert was surprised that he felt so at ease talking to this Gabriel fellow. He didn't usually discuss his life with Bertha with just anyone. In fact, he never discussed it with anyone. "Ever since I first met her back in the second or third grade, I don't remember which, she has pretty much called the shots in our relationship."

"That must not be easy for you."

"Well, I've sort of gotten used to it."

"Even so, it must be difficult."

"Yes, and lately, what with her wanting to be the President of that women's organization..."

"Women Hoping For Equality Now?" Gabriel interrupted.

"Right. She has gotten much more difficult to get along with. Somehow I think she isn't getting what she wants there, in the group."

"It would seem that way, since no one showed up for her dinner last night. That must have really made her angry."

"Livid would be a better word." Hebert laughed, in spite of himself. "And she stormed out of the house this morning heading for the city. But, how is it you know so much about all of this?"

"Councilman Humble, you're a good man." Gabriel said, ignoring Hebert's question. They were at the entrance to the Mall.

"And that means a lot in this world, today. And I think things may get better for you, soon. Have a good day." The tall man shook his hand again and walked away.

"Things may get better for me soon?" Hebert thought. *"I wonder what he meant by that."*

"I really think it's nice of you guys to come help me get these books unpacked and ready to be shelved." Katie said, as she was cutting open another of the packing boxes. "But won't they be missing you down at City Hall?"

"It's quiet down there this morning." Jim answered. "And Paul thought we should come give you a hand."

"Yes, these books can be heavy." Paul said, as he turned red from embarrassment. "And besides, we're almost done."

Katie knew how much Paul liked her. And she felt the same about him. But he was so shy it was almost painful. They had been going to the movies together every Saturday night for weeks before he ever held her hand. And they hadn't progressed to a good night kiss on the porch yet. Katie was sure she would have to take that matter into her own hands.

"This is the last box, guys."

"Gee, that's too bad." Paul said, before thinking, and then turned even redder.

"Listen you two," Jim looked up from unpacking the box he was working on. "Since we're almost done here I'm going down to the coffee shop and pick up some cinnamon buns to take back to the office. Jayne loves them."

"Oh, and you don't?" Katie laughed.

"Any excuse works for me. See you at the office, Paul." Jim called as he left the store.

Katie and Paul worked in silence after Jim left. They took the last books from the packing boxes and stacked them on the book cart. Then they piled the cartons at the back of the store.

"I'll take these out back after Hebert gets here." Katie said.

"Well, I guess that's all you need for me to do so I'll be heading back to City Hall." Paul turned to leave.

Katie put her hand on his arm. "Paul, thanks for helping. I like it when you're around."

Paul's face began to turn red again. "I like being around you, too, Katie."

"Would you like to come to dinner Sunday after Church?" Katie knew her Mom wouldn't mind. She liked Paul a lot.

"Gee, that would be great." Paul said. Any chance he could get to spend more time with Katie he took it. "But, you're sure your Mom won't mind?"

"No, it's okay. Sunday afternoons are kind of boring since my Dad died so we will both appreciate having someone there to laugh with."

"I'll be there." Katie still had her hand on Paul's arm and he wasn't eager to have her take it off. "Your Mom's a great cook."

"Good. About 1:00 then?"

"Okay. Uh, do you suppose I could walk you home after church. If the weather's okay."

"I would like that." Katie said as she leaned over and kissed him on the cheek. Now his face was really red.

Just then Hebert entered the store. "Good Morning, Katie." He called. "Oh, hello Paul. How come you're not at work?"

"Hello, Mr. Humble." Paul welcomed the interruption. "Things were quiet down at City Hall so Jim and I thought we would come help Katie with these books that came in. But I'm outta here now. See you, Katie, Mr. Humble."

"So long, Paul." Hebert said as Paul headed out the door.

"You know, Katie, I think that boy likes you."

"You noticed."

"Couldn't help it." Hebert said, as he began to work on the stack of books. "I don't suppose the feeling is mutual?"

"Mr. H. I really like Paul, a lot. But he is so bashful."

"Paul's a nice young man. And someday he'll get over that bashfulness."

"I just hope he doesn't take too long. I'm not getting any younger, you know." And they both laughed.

****

Rufus Pettifogger wasn't happy. Things had not gone well at the City Council meeting, if you could call nearly being sacked by Pastor Brown not going well. That had been a very scary moment for Rufus as Pastor Brown outweighed him by at least a hundred pounds. *"I should have stood up to him."* Rufus thought. *"I had the Constitution on my side. The separation of Church and State is very clear. At least to me"* Rufus had to keep reminding himself of that fact.

Rufus Pettifogger had been the OARD representative in Newton's Mill ever since the town began to grow. He was sent in by the big city Chapter to monitor perceived violations of anyone's civil liberties and this Nativity Scene situation was just the thing for him to make a name for himself in the Organization. And Rufus desperately wanted tomake a name for himself. His attempts at becoming a respected lawyer never seemed to materialize and he found himself with one hopeless case after another.

When he heard that the OARD was looking for someone to

represent them in Newton's Mill he jumped at the chance. He had visited the little town once before while researching a case, and even though he lost the case, he liked the town. But he was surprised to find that the town had grown much larger, and that OARD felt it was an important to their fight against the celebration of Christmas. It had come to the attention of the organization that the Nativity Scene, displayed on the courthouse lawn, was definitely a violation of the separation of Church and State.

But right now things were not going too well for him. His little run-in with Pastor Brown on Tuesday had made him even more of a laughing stock around town than he was before. And, as he sat in his little office just across the street from City Hall, he was struggling to determine his

next course of action.

"I guess I will have to join with Ira Freethinker and his assistant Phil in order to make a difference." He spoke out loud. "At least we have the same agenda. Between the three of us we might be able to turn this whole situation our way."

Thumbing through the stack of business cards in his top desk drawer he fished out Ira's card, picked up the phone and dialed the number. After three rings he found himself being transferred to voice mail. He left a message for Ira to call him and hung up the phone. He turned back toward his desk from the window and was surprised to find someone standing just in the doorway.

"Can I help you?" He asked.

"Your Rufus Pettifogger?"

"Yes, that's me."

"Local Representative of the OARD?"

"I am, and who might you be?"

"The name's Gabriel." The man said as he came in and took a seat across the desk from Rufus.

"And what can I do for you Mr. Gabriel?"

"It's not Mr., its just Gabriel."

"Oh. Well then, Gabriel, what can I do for you?"

"Wanted to talk to you about last Tuesday night."
"Tuesday?"

"Yes, the City Council meeting."

"Ah yes, and the Nativity Scene flap."

"Exactly."

"And?"

"We're you serious when you called the celebration of Jesus' birth an ethnic folk festival?"

Rufus wasn't sure he wanted to have this conversation right now. "Yes, I was."

"How did you come up with that idea?"

"I was simply making a point."

"A point?"

"Yes, a point that the celebration of Christmas is a folk tradition, nothing more."

"Do you really believe that?"

"Yes, yes I do."

"So then, you are denying two thousand plus years of history, millions of Christians worldwide, and Jesus Christ, Himself?"

"Uh, well." Rufus could see that he was in well over his head with this stranger. "I suppose you could say that, yes."

"Then I ask you again. Do you really believe that?"

Rufus sat quietly for a moment. He had never been asked a question like this before. He was being asked to declare his feelings about Jesus Christ. Somehow he hadn't thought that this Nativity Scene situation was really about Jesus. To him it was just another effort to "undermine traditional values," as the director of the group used to say. But, was he ready to deny the existence of

Jesus, and His birth.

"I see you're having some trouble with the question." Gabriel said. "Well, take your time, you don't have to answer right now. It really is a question that you will have to decide, however, sooner or later."

"I guess I just never looked at it in quite that way." Rufus was reluctant to show his indecision, but this stranger had a way about him. He was strong, but with a gentleness that made Rufus feel uncomfortable and calm, at the same time.

Gabriel stood up to leave. "Well, Rufus, sooner or later you will have to answer that question for yourself." And he turned and walked out of the office.

Rufus sat silently, still struggling with the question.

****

The intercom buzzed on the Mayor's desk.

"Yes, Jayne, what is it." He said, pushing the talk button.

"Mary Beth Johnson's on line one for you."

"Thanks." G.D. picked up the phone and punched the first button. "Hello, Mary Beth, what's up?"

"Just wanted to run something by you. Get your feelings."

"Shoot."

"I want to run an historical piece in Sunday's paper on the origins of the Nativity Scene here in Newton's Mill. Maybe give some folks a little perspective on the whole picture."

"Sounds like a great idea, Mary Beth, what do want from me?"

"Your Dad used to work at the Mill, didn't he?"

"Him and my Granddad, too. We go back a long way with the Mill. I suppose if it was still open I wouldn't be Mayor. I'd be working in the Mill, just like them."

"Do you remember when the Mill closed?"

"Sure do. It was a sad day for this town. I was just fresh out of high school and gettin' ready for the service. Wanted to join before I got drafted."

"Drafted?"

"Sure, don't you remember back in those days every male over the age of 18 had to register and serve at least two years in the military?"

"That's right. It's been so long I had forgotten."

"Anyway, nearly the whole town turned out for the last day. There were a lot of tears in the crowd. Whole generations of folks grew up working in that Mill. Colonel Newton gave me my first job as a kid."

"Really?"

"Yeah, I worked on the cleanup crew after school and on Saturdays. It was a great job for a kid in school."

"Come to think of it, I remember my Brother working there for awhile before he went off to the University."

"Yeah, I think nearly every boy in this town worked there at one time or another. The Colonel was really good about that. If a boy needed work he could always find something for him to do. But I think we're rambling here. What was it you wanted to know about the Mill?"

"When the Mill closed and they were cleaning it out and getting ready to tear it down what happened to the Nativity Scene?"

"It just showed up on the Court House lawn the next Christmas."

"Just showed up?"

"Yeah. I think the fella that made it, Floyd Carver, had died before the Mill closed but someone from his family must have taken it for safekeeping. It was probably one of them that put it there. Then after Christmas, the Mayor, that was old Jed Garner, had it stored in the basement of City Hall. That's where it's been ever since."

"Who puts it up every year?"

"Oh, I just have Sam do it, now. He enjoys getting it set up and the lights put out there. Says it makes it feel more like Christmas."

"Well, what else can you tell me about it?"

"Let's see. When the Mill was active everybody in town would meet there on Christmas Eve and sing carols, the Ladies Auxiliary from the Pastoral Society would have hot cider and little cakes. It was quite an evening. Don't think anybody in town missed it if they could help it."

"Right. My folks used to take me there for that."

"It was quite a nice time."

"Shame we don't do it anymore."

"That it is. But, as the town got bigger those little things seem to disappear. I do miss it."

"Want to give me a scoop on how you're gonna vote Tuesday night?" Mary Beth laughed.

"I would if I knew how I was going to vote. It's not a simple as it seems."

"I know, G. D. Don't want to put you on the spot. It was easy for me to vote. I'm not up for election next year. But Hebert and J.B. are probably going to run again."

"You think so?"

"Sure. Archie loves being a Councilman, and Bertha will push

Hebert into it whether he wants to or not."

"Well, I haven't decided on whether I'll run again. Whatever I decide on this Nativity Scene some folks aren't gonna be too happy."

"Can't please everybody, G.D. Just do what you think is right. Talk to you later."

"So long, Mary Beth. Good talking to you." G. D. placed the phone back on the cradle and swung his chair around to look out the window. *"Just do what I think is right? I wish I knew what that was."*

****

"So, Sam thinks a walk might give me some inspiration for my Sunday sermon." Pastor Brown thought as he walked along. *"Well, I've walked about an hour now and so far nothin' is coming to me. I need your help, Lord."* Artemis was just on the edge of the park. *"Maybe if I sit in the park for awhile that Angel Sam was talkin' about will find me."* Artemis laughed out loud at that.

He walked over to a bench between two trees and sat down. Closing his eyes he began to pray. *"Father, you know I need a good sermon for Sunday. And you always give me the words to say. But, for some reason or other, they're just not gettin' to me today. I really need your help and inspiration. Amen."*

"Hello, Pastor Brown."

"Huh." Artemis jumped. He hadn't heard the stranger sit down next to him.

"Looked like you might be praying. So I was quiet as I could be so as not to disturb you."

"I appreciate that. Yes, I was praying. Asking the Lord for a little help with my Sunday sermon."

"Not going too good?"

"Nope. Just can't seem to hit on a subject. I finished my series on the life of Paul the Apostle last week and have to have something new for this Sunday." Artemis shook his head. "Sam, my wife, suggested I take a walk and maybe God would send an Angel to give me my sermon."

"Any results yet?" The stranger laughed.

"Not so far."

"Well, I was at the City Council meeting last Tuesday night and it would seem to me that there's a subject or two there for a sermon."

"You mean the Nativity Scene?"

"Yep, for starters. I heard you take off after that OARD fella. You sure had plenty of passion there."

"Well, did you hear what he said?"

"I did."

"I wasn't about to let him get away with calling the birth of our Lord and Savior an ethic folk festival. He's lucky he sat down when he did." Artemis stopped. "I'm sorry. Sometimes the old man dies hard. My temper gets away from me once in awhile."

"Oh, that's okay. God's messengers have had to lose their temper a time or two if I remember correctly. Moses comes to mind."

"And rightly so. The people had turned from God and were worshipping idols."

"Sort of like today."

"Excuse me?"

"I said it's sort of like today. Folks are into worshipping things. Idols can be anything, you know."

"You're right. I see so much of it every day. Just a look at J.B. Nickels store about this time of year tells you pretty much what he worships. I saw it when I was playing pro football. Guys were into all sorts of things. Big fancy cars, big fancy houses and fancy women. And the money it took to have all that."

"So, why did you leave it?"

"Because it wasn't me. I grew up here in Newton's Mill. For awhile the fame and money was great. But there was always something missing. Something I needed that just wasn't there."

"So you gave it all up?"

"I did. I walked away from it and never looked back. I found the one thing that I was missing."

"And that was?"

"Jesus. I just needed Him in my life. And I needed to tell others about him. So that's why I became a Pastor. And now I'm sitting here trying to figure out a sermon for Sunday that will make people realize they need Him in their lives."

"Seems to me this whole Nativity Scene conflict is a pretty good illustration of what you were talking about."

"How's that?"

"Well, a lot of folks want the Nativity Scene out of sight. Like they want Jesus out of sight. If they can't see Him then they don't have to think about Him. They might call it separation of Church and State but what it really is is a separation of man from God."

"That's a great point there, my friend. Separation of man from God. Never quite looked at it that way."

"Well, Pastor Brown. That just might be a good subject for your sermon this Sunday. I can't wait to hear it." The stranger got up to leave.

"Wait a second, friend. I don't even know your name."

"It's Gabriel, Pastor Brown. Just Gabriel."

Artemis watched the tall stranger as he walked away. *"Gabriel,"* he said. *"Gabriel, God's messenger. Maybe Sam was right."*

Artemis headed towards his home with the sermon already forming in his mind.

****

Bertha spent the day basking in the activity, the vitality, the excitement of a big city. *"Newton's Mill is so beneath me."* She thought. *"In the city here I could be somebody. Not some dinky bookstore owner's wife, or the President of a club of socially inept women. I could have prestige, status. I belong here."*

Bertha checked into the big hotel near downtown. Went up to her room and called her home number. She knew Hebert wouldn't be home from work yet. She didn't want to talk to him anyway. When the answering machine picked up her call she left a message that she would be spending the night in the city and would be home tomorrow. Then she ordered room service, kicked off her shoes and sat back on the couch that faced the window.

The idea was set in her mind now. She knew just what she had to do.

****

FRIDAY

Friday in the fall around Newton's Mill meant football. Since the town had grown so much in the past few years there were now two High Schools in town, and another one soon to be finished. This made for a pretty exciting rivalry between them. Newton's Mill High was the oldest in the city but, because the other High School was built in an area that had seen huge growth, it was now the underdog in most of the games with the other school. And probably would be when the third school was finished. But this year was a little different. Newton Mill had lost heir coach at the end of the season the year before, and had trouble finding anyone to replace him.

Then someone had the great idea of asking Pastor Brown if he wouldn't mind stepping in as the temporary coach until a regular coach could be found. Artemis thought he might like that and so, with the beginning of practice in the fall he began coaching the team. Now Artemis was a strong man, the terror of opposing backfields. And he brought the same kind of passion to his coaching that he brought to his sermons. At first the players felt intimidated by him but they soon learned that he was fair, and he had a lot to teach them. But the big surprise for the players was that Pastor Brown began every practice session with a prayer for safety for each of his players. It seemed to set the tone for the practices and the team responded by practicing harder than ever. No one wanted to let Artemis down.

The first game of the season was against Barnett High from a town to the west of Newton's Mill. They had pretty much dominated the games because they were a much larger school. But to everyone's surprise Newton's Mill won the game. And to everyone's surprise the players all knelt with the coach, on the field, in front of the stands, and prayed. Thanking God for safety for each of the players and for the other team as well.

That set the tone for the season. Newton's Mill won the next five games on the schedule. They didn't beat anyone badly, mostly because coach Brown substituted freely, giving everyone a chance to play. But they won them. And folks around the High School were getting excited.

****

"Hey, Pastor Brown, or should I call you Coach Brown today?" It was the tall fellow, Gabriel, who had been so helpful the day before.

"I answer to either one, today. How are you Gabriel?" Artemis said, as he was raking up the last of the leaves in his front yard.

"Just fine. How's your sermon coming?'

"Thanks to you it's coming along quite nicely. But, I need to ask you a question."

"Sure, Pastor. What is it?"

"Well, I have to ask you about your name."

"What about it?"

"Gabriel means God's Messenger."

"I know."

"So, are you?"

"Am I what?"

"Are you God's messenger?"

"Now, why would you ask me that?"

"Because I don't think it was just a coincidence that you sat down next to me on that bench yesterday just after I finished praying for some help with my sermon."

"You don't, eh?"

"No. See, I believe God hears my prayers."

"I'm sure He does."

"And that's why I'm asking the question. Are you God's

messenger?" Artemis said with a smile.

Gabriel stood quietly for a minute before answering. "You know how it says in the Bible to show hospitality to strangers?"

"For some who have done this have entertained angels, without realizing it. I know the scripture. Hebrews 13:2."

"Well then, I guess that might be an answer to your question. And then again, it might not be. Good luck tonight." And Gabriel turned and walked away, leaving Pastor Brown to consider what he had heard.

****

"Big game tonight, Mr. Mayor." It was Sam the custodian sweeping off the steps of City Hall.

"That it is. Both the teams are undefeated. Artemis has sure done wonders with the team this year."

"You know what I like about the team?"

"What's that, Sam?"

"You know my Grandson Jared plays safety."

"Right. He's good, too."

"Well, I tried for a long time to get him to come to church with me and he always balked. Had one excuse or another. But since Pastor brown has taken over the team he goes with me every

Sunday. I like the faith that Artemis brings to the team. You know they pray before and after every game?"

"Well, I've seen them pray after the games on the field but I didn't know they prayed before."

"They do. They pray for themselves, and the other team, that no one gets hurt and that everyone plays a clean game. It's made a real difference in Jared."

"You know, come to think of it, I see most of the team members in Church every Sunday morning."

"That's right. Except for the fellows that are Catholic but I hear they all go every Saturday night to Mass as well."

"That speaks well for Pastor Brown and his influence on the boys."

"You know who else it speaks well for?"

"Who?"

"God. Got to get back to work, Mr. Mayor. See you at the game tonight."

G.D. turned and went through the doors into City Hall. *"I guess it really does speak well for God."* He thought.

****

Bertha rose early. She had lots to do today. This was the

beginning of the first day of her new life. "Goodbye Newton's Mill. Hello big city" She said aloud as she began to run water for her bath.

****

Hebert got the message from Bertha when he got home from the store. This wasn't the first time Bertha had not come home from various places that she had gone so he didn't think it too unusual. "She probably wanted to take in a show or something." He thought. "She does love the city."

Hebert ate a light supper, read the paper, took a shower and watched a little TV before going to bed. He slept soundly and woke refreshed. Something about not having Bertha in the house to pick on him that made life easier.

"I shouldn't be thinking like that." He told himself. "Bertha is my wife, for better or for worse. That's what the vows said. And that's how it is."

He made himself a bowl of cereal with a piece of toast and a cup of coffee. As he sat at the table he turned on the little radio that sat on the counter. Bertha didn't like it when he listened to the news in the morning. She didn't like much of anything Hebert did.

"Tonight's the big game between Newton's Mill and Central High." The announcer on the radio said. "Both teams are undefeated and it looks like it's going to be a great game."

Hebert had forgotten that there was a big game tonight. He always liked to go, even though Bertha usually figured out some reason to keep him home.

"Coach Artemis Brown has done a great job with the Newton's Mill team and they should give the big boys from Central a run for their money." The announcer continued. "Kickoff is at 8:00, with the Jayvee game starting at 6:00. Let's all get out and cheer for our favorite team."

"Artemis has done a great job with the team this year." Hebert agreed. *"I like the way he has them pray after every game. But I'll bet Rufus Pettifogger doesn't. I'm surprised he hasn't tried to put a stop to that. Unless he's afraid of Artemis."*

Hebert finished his breakfast, rinsed his dishes in the sink and got his coat from the hall closet. As he drove down to the store he remembered his conversation with the fellow named Gabriel the day before. *"Things will get better for me, soon. That's what he said, but I still don't know what he meant."*

****

J. B. Nickels wasn't a fan of Friday night football. He usually kept the store open until 9:00 each night but it was a waste of money on Friday since nearly everybody went to the game. Making it the worst shopping night of the week during football season.

"Then after football it's basketball." He always complained. "Friday nights are just a bust."

"More coffee, dear?" Cora asked. She was used to hearing him complain about Friday and football so she didn't pay much attention to him. "How are the new Santas working out?"

"Worst crop ever." He growled. "Not a decent Santa in the bunch."

"You say that every year, J. B. but I notice the toy sales still do well. And there's always a line of kids waiting to sit on Santa's lap. So they can't be too bad."

"I had an interesting conversation yesterday with a newcomer to town."

"Oh?"

"Yes, really tall fellow. He had tried out for the Santa job but I didn't pick him."

"Why not?"

"Well, he just didn't seem like the Santa type."

"You mean he wasn't intimidated by you?" Cora knew her husband all too well.

"He came up to me in the coffee shop." J. B. ignored Cora's remark. "He wanted to talk about the Nativity Scene. Asked me why I voted against it."

"What did you tell him?"

"I said I voted against it because it didn't..."

"Because it didn't generate any sales for the store." Cora finished his sentence.

"Well, yes, that's more or less what I told him."

"At least you were truthful."

"But he said something strange just before he walked away."

"Something strange?"

"Yes, he said 'You can't take it with you'."

"You can't take it with you?"

"That's right. What do you suppose he meant by that? I'm not planning on going anywhere. And what is it I can't take?"

"Well, I guess you can't take anything." Cora knew what Gabriel meant. For years she had been trying to get J. B. to be more generous with the money they had. It was like pulling teeth. So, Cora donated to several charities in the name of the store. Since she did the bookkeeping J. B. never knew. And she always asked them not to mention where the money came from.

"Now you sound just like him."

"Alright, J. B. let me put it this way. Nobody lives forever. When you go, all your money stays here."

He had heard this before, from Cora. Every time she wanted to support this charity, or that cause, she always said making money wasn't any good if you couldn't do good with it. But she had never said it quite this way. He didn't like the way this conversation was going.

"I'm not planning on leaving anytime soon."

"I know that, dear. But we have more money than we need. We have no children to leave it to. So why don't we make use of it while we're here?'

J. B. got up from the table. "I don't want to discuss this anymore. This conversation is over. I'm going to work. Come down as soon as you're ready." And he grabbed his coat and left.

Cora sat quietly, sipping her coffee as she heard her husband drive off. *"This Gabriel has really got J. B. upset. I think I would like to talk to him myself."*

****

"Mr. Pettifogger."

"Yes, what it is?" Rufus looked up from his desk.

"I'm Ira Freethinker and this is my assistant Phil Faithless. We represent the Atheists and Agnostics Association. May we come in?"

Rufus knew who these two were. Even though they were sometimes on the same side in a few things he didn't like them much. "Yes, come in. Sit down."

Ira and Phil took chairs across from the desk.

"Now, what can I do for you?"

Well, sir. We thought that our two organizations might pool our resources and abilities to oppose the placing of the Nativity on the Court House lawn."

"What do you suggest?'

"We thought that a few ads in the Newton Mill Press stating our case for the removal of the Nativity from government property would be very effective. And, with our two organizations behind them we could make an impact on the whole issue."

"I see. And just what sort of ads did you have in mind?"

"We thought an ad or two outlining our campaign for the separation of Church and State for starters. Followed by a general refuting of the whole virgin birth myth, and denying the existence of God. They could be very powerful."

Rufus sat quietly for a minute. Gabriel's words were still fresh in his mind from the day before.

"So, you want to run an ad calling the virgin birth a myth and the existence of God a lie. Those are pretty strong statements. Do you think they will do anything other than create more animosity for your organization?"

"That will not deter us, sir. We have the courage of our convictions and intend to vigorously oppose this blatant misuse of government property. Will you join us? The unified front of both our organizations will carry great weight."

Rufus wasn't sure that he wanted to be a part of this ad campaign. In fact, remembering what Gabriel had said, Rufus was having some second thoughts about his whole involvement in this situation.

"Gentlemen, I'm afraid I have to decline your offer. While my organization opposes the placing of religious symbols on government property we do not deny the existence of a higher being. So, becoming a party to your ad campaign would not be in our best interests."

Ira was disappointed. He was sure he could talk Pettifogger into joining his campaign.

"But you do agree that the Nativity Scene has to removed from the Court House lawn?"

"I do. What I don't agree with is your idea that there is no God. So, we seem to be at odds on this question."

"But..." Ira tried to continue.

"I'm sorry. I'm afraid we have nothing further to discuss. Now, if you will excuse me I have some important phone calls to make." Rufus came from behind the desk as Ira and Phil stood up. He guided them toward the door and closed it softly behind them. Then he went back to his desk and sat gazing out of the window.

"I have to think this thing through." He thought. *"Suddenly everything isn't as clear in my mind as it used to be."*

****

Ira and Phil were confused. They thought for sure that Rufus would jump at the chance to strike a blow for their cause.

"Well," Phil said. "That didn't go real well."

"I don't understand it. After the Council meeting I was sure the OARD would be behind us."

"Did it seem to you that Mr. Pettifogger was somewhat uncomfortable?"

"Well, now that you mention it he did seem rather in a hurry to get us out of his office."

"So, now what do we do?" Phil asked.

"I suppose we will just have to go to the newspaper ourselves and place the ad. Without the financial backing of the OARD we won't be able to buy as large an ad."

"How much money do we have for this?"

"Not much. You know the Association is not well funded in this area."

"Oh?"

"Yes, it seems that there are more of them than there are of us."

"Them?"

"Believers, Phil. Believers. In this area there are not many members of the AAA."

"Really? Just how many of us are there?"

"Not too many."

"I know, you said that. But how many are there?"

"Two." Ira answered.

"Two!!!!"

"Just you and me, Phil. We're it."

"That's pitiful. I thought this was a big organization, with lots of members. And you tell me it's just the two of us?"

"This is a small town, Phil. There are many more members in the bigger cities."

"And just what sort of impact do you think the two of us will have if we're the only ones?"

"Phil, don't get discouraged. We're not a large group right now. But after our ad campaign I'm sure we will find others who feel the same as we do."

"And if we don't?"

Ira couldn't answer. He wasn't sure just what they would do.

****

"Good Morning, Mr. Mayor." Jayne said as G.D. entered the office. "I saw you talking to Sam on the steps." "Yes, he was telling me how much he appreciates Artemis' efforts with the football team." G. D. answered. "He really likes the praying before and after the game. Says his grandson has even started going to Church with him on Sunday."

"I know. My cousin Charlie plays on the team, too."

"Really? I didn't know that."

"Yes, and it's made a big difference in him also." Jayne smiled. "My Aunt is amazed at the change. Charlie was a pretty wild kid until he made the team. Reverend Brown has made a big impression on him."

"Well, Artemis is good at making big impressions on people. He impressed a lot of running backs when he played pro ball."

"I sort of hope the school doesn't find another coach. I would like to see Reverend Brown continue in the job. I think it would be good for the team, and the school."

"Not sure that will happen, Jayne. You know Artemis is a pretty busy man, and I just wonder how much coaching gets in the way of leading the Church."

"I have noticed one thing about him."

"What's that?"

"Since he started coaching the team he seems to have a lot more energy. And his sermons on Sunday are getting better all the time. It's like the job has fired him up."

"Come to think of it, I've noticed a difference, too." G.D. started for his office.

"What's on the agenda for today, Jayne?"

"Let's see," Jayne picked up a few papers from her desk. "There's a couple of calls you have to make, J. B. Nickels would like to see you this afternoon..."

"J. B.?" The Mayor interrupted. "What does he want?"

"Not sure. But you can bet it has something to do with the vote on the Nativity Scene. That seems to be all anyone is talking about lately."

"You can say that again. I can hardly go anywhere in town without getting into a conversation about it with someone or other. What else?"

"The Booster Club wants to make sure you're coming to the game tonight. And Hebert Humble called to tell you that he has that book you ordered. Came in yesterday."

"Ah, well, that's not such a bad start for the morning. Give Hebert a call and tell him I'll come by this afternoon to pick it up."

"Right, Mr. Mayor. Oh, and one other thing."

"Yes?"

"Eloise Simonet called to apologize for Bertha Humble's phone call the other day. She said she was shocked at Bertha's attitude."

"Hmm, that sounds like all might not be as it seems with the W.H.E.N. group. I thought Bertha was in line to take over the Presidency from Eloise this year."

"So did I. But it sounded to me like there was a little dissatisfaction with that idea."

"Well, you know Bertha has all the tact of a locomotive. I'm not surprised at most anything she does."

"Poor Hebert." Jayne said. "I'm amazed that he puts up with her the way he does."

"I've known Hebert all my life. And he has always been a gentle soul, with a good heart."

"So how did he get hooked up with Bertha?"

"It was her idea. When Bertha sets her sights on something, or someone, she usually gets her way. Hebert didn't stand a chance. She started running him from their senior year in school and after graduation she just dragged him to the altar. He was too nice a guy to protest, and she was too strong willed for it to do him any good anyway."

"I guess Bertha had some money, as well?"

"Yes. Her Dad inherited a bunch of money from his father, and when Bertha's Dad died it all went to her."

"What about her Mom."

"Didn't get a penny."

"What?"

"Yes. Bertha's Dad left the money to Bertha with the stipulation that she use it to care for her Mom. But her Mom died about six months after her Dad. Some folks thought she died of a broken heart. They were very much the loving couple."

"Looks like none of it rubbed off on Bertha."

"Not much of the loving part, anyway. I think Hebert is a lot stronger than most folks give him credit for though."

"Seems he would have to be to put up with Bertha all these years." Jayne agreed. "But with all her big ideas I'm surprised that she still lives here in Newton's Mill."

"Yes, she does seem more suited for the big city." G. D. took the papers from Jayne and started for his office. "Oh well, on with the day."

****

Things were not going well for the Santas at J. B. Nickels department store. With the steady stream of unruly and difficult kids and the stress of being under the constant scrutiny of J. B. himself they were less than jolly. In fact, two had quit in the last two days and J. B. was looking at the possibility that there would be no Santas left by Christmas. So it was with some concern that J. B. pulled into his reserved parking spot

just outside the main entrance to his store, got out and made his way to his office. On the way he spotted Finster, his hapless assistant, standing near the Santa area.

"Finster!" He called. "I want to see you in my office."

"Yes, J. B." Finster knew that couldn't be good. J.B. only called you into his office to fire you. And he knew that the situation with the Santas was making J.B. very nervous.

J. B. stormed into his office, followed closely by Finster, and sat down at his desk.

"Close the door behind you, Finster." He ordered.

"Yes J. B." Finster did as he was told.

"Sit." J.B. said, pointing to a chair in front of the desk.

"Yes, J. B." Finster sat.

"How many Santas do we have left?"

"Four, J. B." Finster stammered. "Just four. And the one on duty right now is looking really disgusted. I give him another hour and he'll be gone, too."

"What's the matter with these guys? Don't they know what a great job they have?"

"Yeah, a really great job." Finster thought to himself. *"Long working hours, poor working conditions, no benefits and absolute minimum wage."*

"It's a tough job, J. B. Those kids can be brutal." Finster said. "Why, just yesterday one kid kicked Santa because he said he was tired of waiting in line. And another one tried to pull Santa's beard off. Luckily it was the one Santa who has a real beard. But you should have heard him scream."

"Well, that all goes with the territory. Kids are kids. But we have to do something to keep the Santas we have left, or else."

"Or else?"

"Or else you will be pulling Santa duty, everyday, all day." J. B. warned. "So you better figure out some way to keep them."

"But, J. B...." Finster started.

"No buts, Finster. The Santas are your responsibility. Fix it!"

"Yes, J. B." Finster answered. It was no use arguing with him.

"That's all. Get out there and do your job." J. B. pointed to the door.

"Yes J. B." Finster said, as he got up to leave.

"And close the door behind you."

"Yes, J. B."

When Finster had gone J. B. picked up some papers from his desk. It was the sales figures for the past two days. They didn't look good.

"This is dismal." J. B. mumbled to himself. "All the advertising, the Santas, the radio ads, the newspaper ads, and everything else cost money. And we're not making any. This may turn out to be the worst Christmas sale season ever."

J. B. sat back in his chair. *"The way things are going,"* he thought. *"It won't make any difference if I can't take it with me. There won't be anything left to take."*

****

Now Finster wasn't happy. *"Working for J.B. is possibly the worst job in the world."* He thought. *"And trying to ride herd on this crop of Santa losers is really tough. I have to figure out something to do to keep the ones we've got, or I'm gonna be wearing one of those red suits and the scratchy beard and listening to greedy kids all day."*

"Hello, Finster."

"Huh?" Finster hadn't seen the tall man until he spoke to him. "Who are you, and how do you know my name?"

"Don't you remember me? I was here for the Santa auditions a couple of days ago."

"Oh, yeah." Now Finster remembered. "The tall guy who didn't last long."

"That's me." The tall man laughed. "Guess I wasn't what Mr. Nickels was looking for."

"Yeah," Finster mumbled. "You didn't look like a loser."

"You look like something's bothering you." The tall man asked, not bothering to acknowledge Finster's comment.

"Ah, it's nothing. Just a little work problem. And who did you say you were?"

"My name's Gabriel. The trouble wouldn't be with the Santas, would it?"

"Well, now that you mention it, that's just what the problem is." Finster wondered how this fellow knew what was going on. "But how do you know that?"

"Let's just say that it was easy to figure out, since one of your Santas just quit."

"What?" Finster shouted. "Quit?"

"Yes, he just got up out of the chair, dumped one of the kids off his lap and stormed into the dressing room."

"Oh no. Now there's only three left."

"The way things are going your Santas won't make it to Christmas."

"I know, I know. That's the third one that's quit this week. I have to figure out some way to get them to stay."

"What about paying them more money?"

"Hah! J. B. would never go for that."

"Better working conditions?"

"Hah! J. B. would never go for that, either."

"That doesn't leave much else, does it?"

"Nope. But you wanna know the ironic part?"

"What's that?"

"I don't even believe in Santa Claus. Never have. My folks were always telling me that there 'was a reason for the season' and it didn't have anything to do with Santa, and presents."

"Well, it did have to do with one present. A really big one."

"Yeah, I know. And you wanna know something else?'

"Sure."

"This whole thing over the Nativity Scene. If I had my way it would have never come to a vote."

"Oh?"

"I would have just put it up on the Court House lawn, like we've been doing here in town since I was a little kid, and not care at all who didn't like it."

"But your boss voted against it."

"J. B. Nickels would vote against anything that wouldn't make him a buck, or increase traffic in his store."

"Yes, he does seem to be a man with his eye on the bottom

line." Gabriel said. "And a tough man to work for."

"Oh, he's tough alright. But you want to know something interesting. His wife is just the absolute opposite of J. B."

"Oh?"

"Yes, she's generous, cares about folks who are struggling, and gives plenty to charities all over town."

"Hmm, and just what does J. B. think about that?"

"I'm not sure he knows. Most of the donations are anonymous and since she handles the bookkeeping for the store I guess J. B. never finds out."

"So, she's kind and generous?"

"Yes, very much so."

"Then maybe you should talk to her about your Santa problem."

"What do you mean?"

"Well, if J. B. Nickels is too cheap to raise the Santa's salaries, and improve their working conditions, maybe his wife wouldn't be."

"You know, I never thought about that. She might just be the one to talk to. At least it's worth a shot."

"Good idea, Finster."

"Hey, it was your idea. I just learn fast." Finster laughed.

"And, Finster, one more thing."

"What's that?"

"Keep remembering the reason for the season. It's important."

"Why's that?'

"Because too many people are forgetting it." Gabriel turned and walked away.

****

Things were going better than Bertha expected. Her morning had been spent at the lawyer's office that handled her financial affairs. Then a quick trip to the bank to transfer most of her funds from the little bank in Newton's Mill. She left a small amount for Hebert. *"He will just have to make that bookstore he loves so much support him now."* She thought. *"And after he sells the house he will have a little more money. I don't know what more he could want. I never did like that house, anyway. I'll be glad to be rid of it."*

Then the afternoon was spent with a real estate agent that resulted in her putting down a deposit on a lovely condominium right in the heart of one of the nicest areas in the city. Bertha was pleased with herself. Her break from Newton's Mill, and Hebert Humble was just about completed. *"That little town just isn't big enough for someone with great ideas, like me."* She told herself.

Returning to her hotel room she ordered a nice dinner from room service and then placed a call to Hebert. "Hebert," She said when the answering machine picked up the call. "I will be staying here in the city another night." And with that she hung up. No explanation, no discussion. Just her usual way of dealing with him. She spent the rest of the evening planning her escape.

****

"Artemis." Samantha Brown called from the kitchen. "Lunch is ready. Come and get it before I throw it to the hogs."

"Well," Artemis laughed as he walked into the kitchen. "It's a good thing we don't have any hogs. But if we did they would be pretty well fed if they had to eat your cookin'"

"I'll just ignore that." Sam said. "How's the sermon coming?"

"Pretty much done with it. Been in there putting the finishing touches on it."

"You mean you finally got an inspiration?"

"Well, actually I ran into a fellow in the park yesterday. He kind of helped me get my thoughts together for it.

"Who was it?"

"He's new in town. Said his name was Gabriel."

"Well, there's a great name. And he helped you with your thoughts on the sermon?"

"Yes. Gave me just the direction I needed."

"Doesn't Gabriel mean a messenger from God?"

"Yes. Interesting isn't it. Just when I needed to hear from God along comes this fellow named Gabriel."

"I'm glad he was able to help you with that. Do you suppose he might be able to help you win the big game tonight?"

"I don't think so. That's up to the team."

"So, how do you think the team will do?" Sam loved it that Artemis was coaching the team. He loved football so much and this gave him the chance he needed to get back to it. "Those Central boys are pretty good."

"I know. We will have to play our best game tonight. I think the boys are up to it. But win or lose I want it to be a good game with no injuries to anyone."

"You've been lucky so far."

"No, we've been blessed so far. I really think that the prayer before the game for safety for both teams has made a big difference. And have you noticed that we don't get many penalties?"

"Yes, I have noticed. And most of the penalties are for minor things."

"I just try to make the boys play fair and give it their best. Then, when the game's over, you have nothing to be ashamed of. Sort of like life."

"You know what surprised me?"

"What?"

"The last game. When you all knelt on the sidelines to pray several of the players from the other team joined you. That was neat."

"It was, wasn't it? And a bit unexpected."

"Face it, Artemis Brown. You're a great coach, but your something else, as well."

"And what might that be?" He asked.

"You're a great man. And I just love being your wife."

Artemis walked over to where Sam was standing and wrapped his arms around her. "The feeling is mutual," he said. "You're the best thing that God ever put in my life."

"Mmmff mmf," Sam said with her face buried in Artemis' chest.

"What's that, Honey?" He said, looking down with a big grin.

"I said, can we eat now?" She said as she pulled back. "Before the food gets stone cold."

****

Cora Nickels parked her car at the back of the Mall parking lot, with the other employee's cars and started for the entrance. She always parked in the employee's area since J. B. only allowed one reserved space near the entrance for himself. *"Just another example of my husbands' attitude."* She always said to herself. *"I wish I could get him to be more compassionate. Especially at Christmas."*

"Mrs. Nickels?" It was Finster, J. B.'s assistant. He had been standing just inside the door, waiting for her.

"Good Morning, Alan." She was the only one who called him by his first name. "Can I help you?"

"Yes, Ma'am. I have a problem."

"A problem that you can't go to my husband with?" Cora asked. She knew Finster to be a hard worker, faced with the difficult task of working closely with J. B.

"Yes Ma'am. And I'm sorry to bother you with this but I'm afraid I'm at my wits end."

"That's alright, I don't mind. Just what's the problem?"

"Santa Claus."

"Santa Claus?"

"Yes. The problem is, I can't keep them."

"What?"

"I can't keep them. The working conditions are difficult, the kids are sometimes out of control, but the big problem is money."

"I think I know where you're coming from." Cora answered. "We don't pay them enough. Is that it?"

"Yes Ma'am. I've tried to talk to Mr. Nickels about it but he just won't discuss it."

"Well, I suggest we just don't bother him with the details. Would another few dollars an hour help?"

"I'm sure it would since we only pay them the absolute minimum now."

"Yes, hardly enough to live on these days. I'll make arrangements to increase their salaries by another, oh, let's say, another $3.00 an hour. Would that be good?"

"It sure would and it might make it easier to keep them on the job. As it is we only have three left for the rest of the season."

"My goodness. That's not near enough. We need at least three more or we will be killing off our Santas. Can you talk to some of the one's who have quit and see if you can get them back?"

"Well, with the salary increase I might be able to."

"Alright, I'll take care of the paperwork this morning and the raises should be in their checks at the end of the week."

"Thank you so much, Mrs. Nickels. Now, if you'll excuse me I have to go find Gabriel."

"Gabriel? What's he got to do with this?" Cora asked.

"Well, he saw the Santa when he quit this morning and we talked about the problem."

"And?"

"He suggested that I talk to you, since I told him how you were always helping charities, and those who were having difficulties."

"Oh. He thought I might be an easy touch?" Cora said, smiling.

"No Ma'am. Not at all. He just thought that you would be more understanding of the problem.

"And he was right."

"Well, you go back to your Santa crew and give them the good news. And see if you can talk some of the others into coming back to work. The more Santas we have the easier the workload will be."

"I'm on my way. And thanks again."

"You're welcome, Alan." Cora watched him hurry off. *"So, this Gabriel fellow gave Alan the solution to his problem. Now I really think I would like to talk to this Gabriel."* She thought.

****

"Well, Jayne, I think I'll head home. Did we ever hear from J.B.? He wanted to see me this afternoon." The Mayor said, as he came out of his office.

"Nope. I guess he forgot."

"This time of year is a busy one for him. And if he wanted to talk about the Nativity Scene it's just as well. I'm in no mood to get into that subject."

"Okay, Mr. Mayor. I'm about ready to head out myself."

"Jim and Paul gone home already?"

"Not home. They promised to help serve dinner at the homeless shelter this evening before going to the game. So they left a little early. I hope that's alright."

"It sure is. That's really nice of them to offer to do that."

"Yeah, those two guys don't like to let on to anyone but they're both pretty caring. Always doing something for someone. I guess I'll see you at the game."

"Right. Can you do me a favor and call Helen and tell her I'm on my way home, but I want to stop and pick up some dessert for this evening?"

"Will do, Mr. Mayor. See you later."

"So long, Jayne." The Mayor left the building and began his walk to the bakery that was in J. B. Nickel's Mall. *"Seems like everything in town is at the Mall."* He thought.

When he got to the entrance to the Mall he noticed a Salvation Army bell ringer standing near the door. Reaching into his pocket he pulled out some change and went over and dropped it through the slot.

"Thank you, Mr. Mayor." G. D. hadn't noticed at first but the bell ringer was Gabriel, the man he met in Charley's Place the other day.

"Gabriel?"

"Yep, that's me." Gabriel laughed. "Just out here doing my civic duty and collecting some money for a good cause."

"So, how's it going?"

"Not so good."

"Yeah, that bucket did sound a little empty."

"Empty is the right word. You're only the third person to put anything in it and I've been out here quite a while."

"And only three donations?"

"Sad isn't it?"

"It sure is. Why do you suppose so few folks are giving anything?"

"I just think they're confused."

"Confused?"

"Sure. With all this controversy about Christmas I think people haven't got the Christmas Spirit this year."

"The Nativity Scene situation?"

"Well, that might be part of it. You know, so many people just want to call this the Holiday Season. No mention of Christmas at all. And it sure makes it tough on charities."

"Tough? How so."

"Well, most people don't realize that Christmas is the big fund raising time. If they don't make it now, they don't make it."

"What do you mean they don't make it?"

"It's the money that's given at Christmas that works all year helping the poor, the hungry and the homeless."

"But, don't charities get money from donations all year long?"

"Sure, but without the money they get at Christmas the other donations can't make up the shortage. Charities count on the spirit of giving at Christmas to get enough funds to help others.

So, if they don't get it at Christmas that pretty much makes it tough all year."

"I never thought about that. But it makes sense."

"Well, my shift is over. Time to head back to the center."

"Who is going to take over for you here?"

"Nobody. Seems like we don't have as many volunteers for this as we used to, either."

"That's unfortunate."

"Yes, it is. You know, Mr. Mayor, there's a reason why the spirit of Christmas is giving. But people just seem to have forgotten that Christmas started with a gift. So long, and I guess I'll see you at the game tonight?"

"Wouldn't miss it. So long, Gabriel." G. D. stood watching as Gabriel walked off down the street. *"Christmas started with a gift."* He thought. *"I wonder what he meant by that?"*

****

The big game turned out to be a barn burner. The boys from Central jumped off to a quick lead and were ahead by two touchdowns at the half. Artemis Brown stood in front of his players in the locker room. They had played hard but the Central players were much bigger, and faster. It didn't look good for Newton's Mill.

"It's been a good, hard fought game so far." Artemis began. "And you men have made me proud of you. Now I'm not gonna stand up here and give you some enthusiastic pep talk for the second half. I don't need to. You all know what we have to do. We need to play our game. We need to do the things we've done all year. Take advantage of their mistakes and play the best we know how. Sure, they're a lot bigger and faster than we are. But we've shown we can score on them. So they're not unbeatable. I want you to go back to the basics. Run hard, block clean and make the tackles. We receive the kick this half. Let's go out there and take it in for a score. Show them that they're in a real football game."

"Coach?" It was Sam Barnes Grandson, Jared.

"Yes, Jared?"

"I think we need a prayer before we go back out there."

Several of the other players nodded their approval.
"Alright, Jared. Why don't you pray for us?"

"Me?"

"Sure."

"Well, okay." Jared knelt in front of the lockers, as did the rest of the team. Even the coaches got down on their knees. "Lord, looks like we have a tough job ahead of us. We've done our best so far, but right now we need a little more. We need some help from You. I'm not asking You to let us win. Just let us do our best. We leave the rest up to You. Amen."

"That's it, men. Second half. Let's go."

The team jumped to their feet and ran back onto the field.

****

"Good game, isn't Mr. Mayor?" It was Hebert Humble.

"Hebert, good to see you. Where's Bertha?"

"Oh, she's still in the city. That's why I have the chance to make it to the game tonight."

"Oh?"

"Yes, Bertha isn't too fond of football so she usually has other things for me to do on Friday nights."

"Well, looks like you picked a great game."

"Those fellows from Central are a pretty big bunch." Hebert said. "Our boys look kind of small up against them."

"Yeah, but their only up by two touchdowns. We still have a chance."

"I suppose Artemis will have them all fired up for the second half. He has sure done wonders with the team this year."

"That he has. You say Bertha is in the city?"

"Yes, she's been gone a couple of days now."

"Business?"

"No, I think she just wanted to get away for awhile. You know the dinner party she wanted you to come to?"

"Ah, yes, I remember. I turned her down."

"Well, it seems so did everybody else in the W.H.E.N. organization."

"You mean?"

"Yep, nobody showed up."

"Nobody?"

"Not a soul. I wound up taking the dinner to the homeless shelter that night. She left for the city the next day and all I've heard from her is a couple of messages that she was staying over."

"Is that something she usually does?'

"No, not exactly. Mostly she just goes for the day and comes home in the evening."

"She must have been really upset that no one came to the

party?"

"I think upset is too mild a word. Livid would be more appropriate."

"So, does she have friends in the city?"

"No, she just stays at the Ritz hotel. She says she likes the amenities."

"Somehow I think Bertha isn't too happy with Newton's Mill."

"She's not. But it's her hometown and so I guess she will just learn to get along. But if things don't go well with her election to the organization presidency she will probably be spending a lot more time in the city. I think it's her hiding place."

"Hiding place?"

"Yes, when the going gets tough, she gets going, to the city." Hebert laughed. "I guess that's a little harsh."

"Well, sometimes the truth is hard." G. D. laughed as well. "At least you seem to be taking it in stride."

"What else is there to do? Bertha does what Bertha wants. Always has, always will. I just let her do what she wants. Not that I could do anything to stop her. I'm not exactly the strong silent type, you know." And Hebert laughed again.

"Hebert, I've known you since we were kids. You've always

been a kind and gentle person. I am sure that living with Bertha takes a lot of strength. She is, as we all know, a strong willed woman."

"I suppose I've gotten used to her over the years. But I don't know why I'm dropping all this on you. You have enough troubles of your own."

"Ah, yes. The Nativity Scene."

"Any idea how you will vote?"

"Still working on it. Couldn't tell you anyway, you know."

"Right. Well, I'm sure that whatever you decide it will be the right one. The teams are coming back on the field. I better get back to my group."

"Your group?"

"Yes, Katie Black, her Mom, your two clerks Jim and Paul, and Jayne, your secretary. You know Paul is kind of sweet on Katie?"

"That's putting it mildly. Head over heels would be a better description."

"They make a nice couple. Katie is a real sweet girl. Sort of like the daughter I never had. It's fun being around them. See you later, Mr. Mayor."

"So long, Hebert. Enjoy." G. D. returned to his seat.

"Did I see you talking to Hebert, dear?" Helen asked when he sat down. "I didn't know he ever came to the games."

"Yes. Seems Bertha has been in the city for a couple of days. So I guess Hebert has a little freedom. He's here with Katie, her Mom and my whole staff from City Hall."

"That's nice. I like Hebert."

"Most people do. Bertha doesn't seem to, though."

"And that's unfortunate. That seems like a loveless marriage."

"That might be a little harsh. But there does seem to be a lack of affection on Bertha's part. No wonder Hebert enjoys being with others."

"There's the kickoff." Helen shouted as she jumped to her feet, along with everyone else in the stands.

"This woman really loves football." G. D. thought. *"How lucky can one man get?*

****

Newton's Mill took the second half kickoff and drove down for a score in six plays. The Central team seemed a little disorganized and three plays later Jared intercepted a Central pass and took it in for the score that tied the game. After that it was mostly a defensive struggle. Newton's Mill held the Central boys to just three first downs in the second half and pushed across a score with less than a minute left to win the game. The Newton's Mill fans went wild, but down on the field coach Brown was calling all his team together in front of their bench. They joined hands and knelt in a circle. Soon some of the Central boys came over and joined hands with the Newton's Mill players. The stands grew quiet. One by one, the folks in the stands joined hands and bowed their heads. From the field you could hear Artemis Brown. "Lord, we thank you for a fair game, with no injuries. We praise you for the lives of each of these boys on both sides of the field. They played hard, Lord. And they played fair. There are no losers in this game, Lord, only players who know they played their best, and gave it everything they had. Bless them now, Lord, and may they always play the game of life hard and fair. Amen."

****

When the weather was good, as it was this night, G. D. and Helen liked to walk home from the games. It was only about a mile and a half and they usually stopped for hot chocolate to sip while they walked.

"That was quite a game." Helen said, as they walked. "I sure thought we were gonna lose it."

"Artemis must have fired the team up at half time." G.D. answered. "And I suppose if anyone could do it, he could."

"You know, I thought it was interesting that Hebert was at the game with Katie and the rest. I think he almost looks at her as the daughter he never had."

"That's funny that you should say that. Those were his exact words to me. You know, I don't think Hebert is a happy man."

"I don't suppose being married to Bertha has anything to do with that?"

"Now Helen, don't be cruel."

"Seriously, G. D., we've known Bertha and Hebert since grade school, right?"

"Right."

"And in all those years have we ever known Bertha to be anything but a manipulative, controlling person?"

"Nope."

"We also know that she rules Hebert with an iron hand. He can't really do much of anything unless Bertha says it's okay."

"Yes, and somehow I have trouble understanding how, or why, he has put up with it all these years."

"Because he's Hebert."

"I suppose that does explain it. Some folks are just too gentle for this difficult world."

"I think the bookstore is Hebert's hiding place."

"Now it's interesting that you should say that. Hebert told me that the city is Bertha's hiding place."

"Oh?"

"Yes. He jokingly said that when the going gets tough for Bertha she gets going, to the city."

"I can't imagine the going getting too tough for Bertha."

"Well, evidently it did the other night. She planned a party for all the ladies from the

W.H.E.N. organization. She even invited me."

"You?" "Uh huh, what she wanted to do was put me on the spot about this Nativity Scene and I declined her offer."

"I'm sure that didn't make her happy."

"Especially after she had Hebert prepare this grand dinner…"

"Hebert?"

"She put the whole preparation on him. Anyway, after getting all this ready no one from the organization showed up."

"Now I'll bet that really made her mad."

"Actually livid was the word Hebert used."

"Why did no one show up, do you suppose?"

"I'm not sure. But the interesting thing is Eloise Simonet called me to apologize for the way Bertha acted. So I get the feeling that things aren't going so well for her in the organization."

"Isn't she running for the presidency?"

"Seems so. But I'm not sure just how that is going now. Looks like whatever support she had is evaporating."

"G.D., do you remember when we were kids Bertha said she never wanted to spend the rest of her life in Newton's Mill."

G. D. thought for a minute. "No, when did she say that?"

"Maybe you weren't there. Several of us girls were having lunch together and Bertha invited herself to join us. We were all talking about what a great town we lived in and how much we enjoyed being a part of all that went on here. Well, Bertha just came right out and said she hated Newton's Mill. It was just too small for her and she hoped she would never have to live her whole life here."

"Interesting."

"She said that when she grew up she would live in the big city and do lots of exciting things. We all thought she was just joking, but she was dead serious."

"That would explain why she runs off to the city whenever

things don't go her way, alright."

"G. D." Helen stopped. "Look over there."

The route from the stadium to home passed across the street from J. B. Nickels' Mall, which was closed at this hour. Most of the lights were out in the stores. Across the front of the main entrance were bright red lights spelling out:

CHRISTMAS SALES-CHRISTMAS SALES-CHRISTMAS SALES

These lights were usually turned off when the store was closed but tonight only part of the lights were out. What the Mayor and Helen saw across the front of the entrance was:

CHRIST   IS   CHRISTMAS

"That's odd. Those lights are supposed to be off." "G.D., look at them. Look at what it says."

"Christ is Christmas."

"G.D., I think this was meant for you."

"What do you mean?"

"This was meant to help you decide what to do about the Nativity Scene."

"Well, Hello Mr. Mayor." It was Gabriel. They hadn't heard him come up. "Some game, huh?"

"Yes it was pretty exciting. Oh, Gabriel, this is my wife, Helen."

"Please to meet you Mrs. Mayor."

"Actually, it's Steward." Helen said, as she shook his hand."

"Right. Just a little joke there."

"We were just looking at the lights across the street."

Gabriel looked past them to the entrance. He stood quietly for a moment. "That's very interesting. The truth in big red letters."

"The truth?" Helen asked.

"Why do you think they call it Christmas?"

"Of course, because it's Christ's birthday." Helen answered.

"Too many people seem to have forgotten that. It's nice that we can be reminded of it like this. But I'm sure J.B. had nothing to do with it."

"You can bet on that." G. D. said. "Helen thinks that was there to help me make a decision about the Nativity Scene."

"I'm not sure that's the case. But stranger things have happened. God does work in mysterious ways, they say."

"I guess this whole situation is weighing on me more than I realize." G. D. answered. "I'm sure this is nothing but a coincidence. I can't keep making more of things than they really are."

"Mr. Mayor, this is a difficult world to live in. So many people with so many ideas of

how things should be. Some want God completely out of their lives. Because He's a nuisance."

"A nuisance?" Helen asked.

"It's not easy doing your own thing when you know that there's a higher power to answer to. So if they ignore Him, or say He doesn't exist it relieves them of any feelings of guilt."

"But, it's just a Nativity Scene." G. D. argued. "What's the big deal?"

"It's what it stands for, Mr. Mayor. A precious gift of love. Unconditional love. Some people can't deal with that." "So, what your saying is it's bigger than just a Nativity Scene being on city property?"

"Much bigger. I'm not sure you're aware of it, but this situation is being closely watched by towns and cities across the country."

"WHAT???" The Mayor almost shouted.

"The news about what's at stake here is all over the papers, and TV, and the radio."

"We seldom watch TV and hardly ever listen to the radio." Helen said.

"Well, like it or not, this is a bigger decision than you realized. And it's been a long time coming. Year after year more and more communities are taking Christ out of Christmas. In the schools, the shopping malls, wherever they can. So, the town of Newton's Mill stands as a symbol."

"A symbol?"

"Yes. What you do here will be felt around the country, good or bad."

"Wonderful." G. D. mumbled. "Just what I needed. More pressure."

"I must be going." Gabriel said. "Nice to meet you Mrs. Steward. You folks have a good rest of the evening."

"Good night, Gabriel." Helen said.

"Oh, and Mr. Mayor."

"Yes, Gabriel."

"The answer to all of this is in your heart." And with that he turned and walked away.

G. D. and Helen walked the rest of the way home in silence.

****

Hebert had really enjoyed himself at the game. It was fun being with Katie and the rest. He enjoyed young people. And watching Paul and Katie try to act nonchalant about their relationship while Jim had great fun teasing them all night long was good for several laughs. All in all it had been a great evening. And the win by Newton's Mill just made it just that much better.

Hebert pulled his car into the driveway, being sure to leave enough room for Bertha if she decided to come home early before he left for work. He went inside, made himself a cup of tea and sat down to catch the news on TV before going to bed. He could never do that when Bertha was home. She always demanded complete silence when she went to bed.

"Now for our local news." The announcer said. "It seems the situation with the Nativity Scene and the Court House lawn has become bigger than just Newton's Mill."

"What?" Hebert sat up in his chair.

"Yes," the announcer continued. "Cities and towns all across the country are watching very closely just what happens here in our little town which is not so little anymore. It seems that this controversy has ignited passions on both sides of the issue. For an update on the story let's go to our correspondent at the State Capitol. Julie?"

"Thank you, Wayne. Yes folks it seems that all eyes are on

Newton's Mill. And the battle lines are forming. With me is Reverend William Morgan, pastor of the First Methodist Church here in the capitol. Reverend Morgan what's your take on all this?"

"Well, Julie, I think it's been a long time coming. For too long we have been doing everything we can to take Christ out of Christmas, and turn it into a winter holiday event."

"A winter holiday event?"

"That's right. The reason for this season came over 2000 years ago with a hope for peace and a heart full of unconditional love. And there are some who would bury that beneath a pile of holiday decorations, inane holiday music and so called fantastic holiday sales."

"So, if it were up to you...?"

"If it were up to me I would put that Nativity Scene on the Court House lawn and light it so it could be seen for miles."

"Thank you Reverend. Well, there you have it folks. Just one side of the story. Now to bring you the opposite argument we go to my colleague Harry Clark with the head of the local OARD here at the capitol. Harry."

"Thanks, Julie. With me is Garfield Cummins, head of the OARD here in our state. Mr. Cummins, you heard the Reverend, what's your stand on this?"

"The OARD's stand is as it always has been. No religious symbols on Government Property."

"So, you oppose any and all religious symbols on Government property? Without exception?"

"Without exception. The Constitution is very clear on the separation of Church and State and this is a clear violation of that amendment. Whether it be a cross, a Menorah, or a Nativity scene it all speaks of religion."

"Then I take it that you, yourself are not a religious person?"

"Certainly not. Religion is for the unwashed masses."

"Wait a minute. That sounds like something from an atheist point of view. Are you an atheist, Mr. Cummins?"

"What I am is of no consequence in this discussion."

"Well then, I think you have answered my question. Thank you, Mr. Cummins."

"But..."

"So much for here, back to you, John."

You could see a very agitated Garfield Cummins trying to get a word in before they switched to the local broadcast. Obviously he wasn't too happy with the interview.

"Great, Harry. Looks like there are serious arguments on both sides of this issue. And now, for the weather."

Hebert switched off the TV and sat quietly for a moment. *"Because I voted against the Nativity Scene,"* he thought. *"Do you suppose people think I'm an atheist? You know, when you look at it a certain way voting no on the Nativity scene could be seen as a vote against God."*

Hebert was suddenly very concerned. He definitely wasn't against God. But it had never occurred to him that his vote might be seen that way.

"God," Hebert bowed his head. "You know I would never vote against you. You have been the only thing that has kept me sane through all these years of living with Bertha. Forgive me, Father. I just didn't see things clearly. I didn't realize that the Nativity Scene is really a symbol of what You gave to us so many years ago. It's just sort of become a thing in this world today. I pray that the mayor will make the right decision. I didn't. I hope You will guide him. Amen."

Hebert sat a long while after he prayed. Then he got up, took his cup to the sink, rinsed it out and went upstairs to bed.

****

"It was fun going to the game tonight with everyone, wasn't it Mom?" Katie said as she put on water for tea. "Mr. H. is a lot of fun. I didn't realize he had such a good sense of humor."

"Well, when we were kids in school he was actually known as Happy Hebert."

"Happy Hebert?"

"That's right. He was always telling a joke, cheering someone up, or clowning around in study hall."

"Wow, what happened?"

"Bertha happened. When she set her sights on Hebert his whole demeanor changed. It was as if he was embarrassed to have any fun. And he didn't hang around with the bunch of us anymore."

"When did that happen?"

"Junior year."

"So, Bertha has been an influence on Mr. H. since then?"

"Well, I actually think she started earlier but it didn't begin to show until then."

"You know, I went over to their house the other night to help Mr. H. get ready for a big party that Bertha was going to give. She left him the whole job. So I just figured I could help."

"Bertha was always good at that. Leaving things for Hebert to do. Most of the time she kept him so busy it's a wonder he even had time to study."

"But he told me the next day that nobody showed up for the

dinner."

"What?"

"He said it was supposed to be a dinner for the women from that group she belongs to."

"W.H.E.N.?"

"Yeah, that's the one."

"And nobody showed up?"

"Not even one person."

"So, what happened?"

"Mr. H. said Bertha got really angry and went up to bed. Left all that food and everything."

"So what did he do?"

"He loaded it all up in his car and took it to the homeless shelter."

"That sounds like Hebert. Something funny about tonight, though."

"What's that, Mom?" Katie said as she poured water into their cups.

"The only reason Hebert was able to make it to the game tonight was because Bertha had been in the city the past couple of days."

"So?"

"So I've never known Bertha to leave Hebert alone for even one full day, let alone two. There's something going on there."

"Like what?"

"Bertha has never really liked living here in Newton's Mill. Even as a girl she always said she would never want to live here her whole life. She talked about going to the city to live, but when she and Hebert got married she seemed to settle down. At least as far as living here went."

"But, she wouldn't leave Mr. H., would she?"

"If it suited her purposes she would. In a heartbeat."

"I really hate to see her treat Mr. H. the way she does. Sometimes he comes into the store in the morning and it's a couple of hours before he brightens up. And all it takes is one phone call from her to spoil the rest of his day."

"You know, Katie, I suppose I shouldn't say this, but I think Hebert would be better off if she went to live in the city permanently."

"Mom!"

"I know that sounds awful. But I've known Hebert for most of my life. He and your Dad were close before Bertha came along. And I hate to see him treated the way she treats him. And it seems to get worse every year."

"You know, Mom, it seems that no matter how upset he is, or sad, or preoccupied he always treats me as if I were his daughter. And he loves to see Paul and I together."

"Well, you do make a nice couple. And Paul is a wonderful young man."

"He is, isn't he?" Katie said with a smile.

"That he is. Now you better get up to bed or I'll never be able to get you up in the morning."

"Okay. The excitement of the game really had me revved up but the tea has helped calm me down. So I should be able to sleep."

"The game? Or Paul?"

"Mom!"

"Good night, Katie."

"Good night, Mom." Katie said as she kissed her Mom on the cheek. "You should get some sleep, too."

"I'll be up in a minute."

When Katie had gone her Mom sat quietly, sipping on the last of her tea. On nights like this she really missed Katie's Dad. They had always gone to the games together and would sit here in the kitchen long after they had put Katie to bed, and talk about the game, and other things. "She's turning into a fine young lady, John." She whispered. "You would be so proud of her. I just wish you could be here to see it. I miss you so much."

Wiping a tear from her eye she rose, took her cup to the sink, and turned off the light. As she climbed the stairs to her bedroom she was suddenly very lonely.

****

Bertha turned out the lights and lay looking out the window at the city. *"Tomorrow is the big day,"* she thought. *"Tomorrow is the day I say goodbye to Newton's Mill, and Hebert, and all those small minded people who never have appreciated me. How exciting."*

Bertha pulled the covers up under her chin and fell asleep. The smile was still on her face.

****

"Good night, G.D." Helen leaned over and kissed him. "It was a lot of fun tonight."

"Good night, sweetie. See you in the morning."

Helen was asleep almost immediately. Not so for the Mayor.

The past few days had been difficult and he tossed and turned, trying to clear his mind of thoughts of the Nativity Scene, the pending City Council meeting, the kids getting on him, and Gabriel. *"Just who is this Gabriel fellow,"* he wondered, as he fell into a fitful sleep.

"Mr. Mayor."

"Huh?" G.D. sat up in bed. There, at the foot stood a figure, rather transparent, and a little scary. "Who are you?"

"I'm the ghost of Christmas past."

"Yeah, right, and I'm Ebenezer Scrooge"

"Very funny, Mr. Mayor. But this isn't a time for jokes. I don't have much time, and there is lot for you to see."

"Wait a minute, what are you talking about? And you don't think I really believe this ghost stuff, do you?"

"Believe what you want, but come with me."

Before G. D. knew what was happening he was walking along the Main street of Newton's Mill. But it didn't look like Main Street. Or did it.

"This looks like Main Street when I was a kid." He said to his companion. "Where are we going?"

"You'll see. And you're right. This is Main Street before

Newton's Mill began to grow. Back when the celebration of Christmas was a big part of life here in town. Look up ahead."

G.D. saw the Mill. Looking just like it did when everyone gathered around the Nativity Scene on Christmas Eve to sing carols.

"I remember this. It was always such a special time. Even as a kid it meant a lot to me."

"It meant a lot to all the folks that gathered here. Look around. Tell me what you see."

G.D. stood on the edge of the crowd. There was old Colonel Newton, and his wife. And Judge Carson who was the only judge in town for many years. "And look," He said. "There's old Floyd Carver. He was the one who made the Nativity Scene. I had almost forgotten what he looked like."

As G.D. and his companion stood watching the crowd the sound of Christmas Carols filled the air. There was a feeling of happiness, and peace. And as he looked around he caught sight of Archie, and Helen, and Hebert, and J.B. but they were all just kids. And then he saw himself, standing with his Dad and Mom, gone these many years.

"Mr. Mayor, this is what Christmas was back then. Christmas Carols, the Nativity Scene and good folks gathered together to celebrate a gift. Things that have been forgotten now. A time that was gentle and peaceful."

"But look at it, now." It was another voice. G. D. turned to see another figure, just as transparent as the first, but dressed in modern clothes.

"Who are you?" He asked.

"Christmas Present, and no smart remarks."

When G. D. turned to look back at the scene, it was gone. In its place was J. B. Nickels' Mall, with lights and shoppers and tunes about reindeer and Santa, and jingle bells playing on the sound system. Nowhere could be found any sign of that soft and tender time from before.

"What happened?"

"This is what Christmas has become. It's not the celebration of God's gift. It's a time for buying, and selling, and going into debt to buy things that will be forgotten in a short while. This is Christmas, today. But, they don't call it Christmas much anymore. They call it the Holiday Season."

"You know, you guys aren't making this any easier on me."

"We don't intend to. What you have to decide isn't easy. We just want to help you see things a little clearer."

"Okay, so if I remember the story right the next one of you guys should be Christmas Future. So where is he?"

"He isn't."

"He isn't? What do you mean he isn't?"

"He isn't because if people continue to deny the reason for Christmas soon it will be no more. And, it's all your fault."

"What?"

"It's all your fault, it's all your fault." The two apparitions chanted as the faded out of sight.

"It is not!!" G.D. shouted as he sat up in bed.

"It is not what?" Helen asked, sleepily.

"It's not my fault."

"What's not your fault, dear?"

"Never mind." G. D. got up out of bed. "I'm going downstairs and have a cup of tea. I can't sleep anyway."

"That's nice, dear." Helen said, as she turned over. G. D. stood and looked at her for a minute, then shook his head, put on his robe and went downstairs.

****

Gordon Steward, G. D.'s twelve-year-old son, couldn't sleep either. So he had come downstairs, made himself a glass of chocolate milk, got a couple of cookies from the cookie jar and sat down at the kitchen table. He looked up as his Dad came into the kitchen.

"Gordon, what are you doing up?" G. D. Asked.

"Couldn't sleep, Dad."

"You, too. I was asleep, but a bad dream woke me up and I was having trouble getting back to sleep."

"A bad dream?"

"Yeah, it's this whole Nativity Scene thing. It's really got me spooked. But what's keeping you up?"

"Well, I got a real problem."

"Yeah, that makes two of us. What's the problem? Maybe it will take my mind off what's bothering me."

"I, uh," Gordon wasn't sure just how to tell his Dad.

"C'mon, Son. What's bothering you?"

"It's school."

"What about it?"

"I got in trouble today and I didn't even do anything." Gordon blurted out.

"You don't get in trouble for not doing anything, unless it's your homework."

"Funny, Dad. But I did. And I even got sent to the Principal's office."

"What?"

"I got sent to the Principal's office for asking the teacher a question she couldn't answer."

"And just what kind of question did you ask?" G.D. asked, suspiciously.

"It's nothing like that, Dad. I just wanted to know why we were having a winter carnival instead of a Christmas Pageant this year."

"Wait a minute. You're not having a Christmas Pageant this year?"

"No, they call it a Winter Carnival now. And we can't sing any Christmas Carols, either."

"No Christmas Carols?"

"No, we have to sing stuff like a song about a stupid snowman, or jingle bells, and Santa Claus coming to town. Yucchh. And anyway, Santa Claus has been in town since September at Nickel's department store."

"Yes," G. D. chuckled. "And if old J. B. had his way Santa would be there all year."

"Well, I'm really confused, Dad. And the Principal couldn't answer my question, either. Said something about Board of

Education Policy. What's happening? Why isn't Christmas Christmas anymore?"

"I don't know, Son. Things were a lot simpler when I was your age. At least they seemed to be."

"Do you remember when Grandpa used to read us the Christmas story?"

"Yes, I sure do. He read it to me every Christmas when I was a boy. Just like his Dad read it to him. It was a family tradition."

"You know, Dad. I haven't heard it since Grandpa died."

"You're right, Son." G. D. said, after a long pause. "It has been a long time since I read that story. I guess since Grandpa died I've just sort of let the old family tradition die, too. Maybe now is the right time to bring it back to life. Let's go in the living room."

G. D. and Gordon picked up their milk and cookies and made their way to the living room. G. D. turned on the small table lamp at the end of the sofa, went over to the bookcase and took a well-worn Bible from the shelf. "This was Grandpa's Bible. See how the pages are worn. He always had it within reach and knew just where to turn if he needed help with a problem, or wanted to thank God for some blessing."

G. D. opened the book. "Let's see, I think the verses we want are in Luke 2 Ah yes, here it is." G. D. sat down next to Gordon, who moved closer and sat with his head leaning against his Dad's shoulder. *"Just the way I used to sit when Dad read this to me."* He thought.

"In those days," G. D. began to read. "Caesar Augustus issued a decree that a census should be taken of the entire Roman world. This was the first census that took place while Quirinius was governor of Syria. And everyone went to his own town to register.

"So Joseph went up from the town of Nazareth in Galilee to Judea, to Bethlehem the town of David, because he was of the house and line of David. He went there with Mary, who was pledged to be married to him and was expecting a child. While they were there, the time came for the baby to be born, and she gave birth to her first-born son. She wrapped him in cloths and placed him in a manger, because there was no room for them in the inn.

"And there were shepherds living out in the fields nearby, keeping watch over their flocks at night. An angel of the Lord appeared to them, and the glory of the Lord shone round them and they were terrified. But the angel said to them, 'Do not be afraid. I bring you good news of great joy that will be for all the people. Today, in the town of David a Savior has been born to you. You will find the baby wrapped in cloths and lying in a manger.'

Unknown to G.D and Gordon Helen had heard their voices and had come downstairs to sit on the steps and listen.

"Suddenly a great company of the heavenly host appeared with the angel praising God and saying, 'Glory to God in the highest and on earth peace to men on whom his favor rests.'

When the angels had left them and gone into heaven, the shepherds said to one another, 'Let's go to Bethlehem and see this thing that has happened, which the Lord has told us about.'

So they hurried off and found Mary and Joseph and the baby, who was lying in the manger. When they had seen him they spread the word concerning what had been told them about the child. And all who heard it were amazed at what the shepherds said to them. But Mary treasured up all these things and pondered them in her heart.

"And the shepherds returned, glorifying and praising God for all the things they had heard and seen, which were just as they had been told."

G. D. closed the Bible and sat quietly. At first he thought that Gordon had fallen asleep and didn't want to wake him.

"You know, Dad." Gordon said softly. "I wonder what it must have been like then. Seeing the angels, and going to Bethlehem to see Jesus. It's a wonder when the angels all appeared in the sky that the shepherds didn't all have heart attacks."

"Yes, I imagine that was pretty awesome. It's a good thing the angel came to warn them first. When Grandpa read this to me I always thought about how it must have been for them to see the baby Jesus, and wondering how this little baby could save anybody from anything."

"And Mary. Imagine how she must have felt, looking at Jesus and knowing he was the Son of God."

"Right. being a parent is tough enough. But being the Mom and Dad of God's Son. Well that would really put some pressure on you. They did pretty well, though."

"You do pretty well, too, Dad. It's always nice to know that when I have a problem I can go to my father for help. Thanks for reading the story to me again. I think we should do it every year, just like Grandpa did. Goodnight, Dad. I think I won't have any trouble sleeping now." Gordon got up, leaned down and kissed his Dad on the cheek turned toward the stairs when he saw his Mom.

"Oh, hi, Mom. Have you been sitting there long?"

"Long enough to hear most of the story. My Dad used to read it to me, too, when I was little. I never get tired of hearing it."

"I told Dad we should do it every year."

"That would be good."

"Well, Good night." Gordon headed up the stairs.

"Good night, Son. See you in the morning." Helen stood up and gave him a hug, then went to sit with G.D and the two of them sat quietly for a long while after Gordon left.

"The reading of Luke 2 was good for me," G.D. spoke. "I needed to refresh my memory as to the facts behind the season. But something Gordon said kept coming back to me."

"What was that dear?" Helen asked.

"He said it's always nice to know when I have a problem I can go to my father for help." G.D. said. "Maybe I need to go to my Heavenly Father for a little help." G. D. lay the Bible down took hold of Helen's hand and went to his knees in front of the couch. Helen knelt beside him as he began to speak.

"Lord, it's me, I got a real problem..."

****

Saturday

Hebert hadn't slept so well in years. *"Must have been the fresh air at the football game."* He thought as he rolled out of bed. *"And the peace and quiet around the house the last couple of days."* He added as he went to the bathroom to get ready for the day. His stress level had seemed to be at a low point with Bertha gone. But he wasn't prepared to place the blame on Bertha, at least not totally. As he washed and shaved he thought about the night before and the fun he had with Katie, her Mom and the young men from the Mayor's office. He wondered, again, just what made him tell the Mayor about the difficulty with Bertha and the ladies from the organization. It wasn't like him to discuss family matters with just anyone. But he had known G. D. since they were boys, and the Mayor was always easy to talk to. And, somehow, it made him feel a little better.

After a breakfast of cold cereal, toast and coffee, he grabbed his jacket from the closet, closed the front door behind him and left for work.

****

Bertha watched Hebert leave the house. She had risen early, had a quick breakfast and drove to Newton's Mill. She parked the car just down the street, where she was sure Hebert wouldn't see her, and waited for him to leave.

"There he goes," she thought. *"And he forgot to lock the front door again. It's a wonder we haven't been robbed before this. Oh well, in a few hours that won't be any concern of mine."*

When Hebert had driven down the street and around the corner Bertha started up her car and drove to the house. She used her garage door opener and pulled the car inside, closing it behind her.

She didn't want any of the neighbors to know she was home. She picked up a folder from the seat next to her, got out, went into the house and up the stairs to her bedroom. Taking suitcases from the hallway she began to pack. In a few minutes her closet and dresser were empty.

Bertha carried the suitcases down to the car, opened the trunk and put them inside. She went back into the house and looked around to see if there was anything else she wanted to take with her.

"I have all I want from this house." She said aloud. "Hebert can have everything. I don't want anything that reminds me of this house, this town or the miserable years I have spent here."

Picking up the folder from the coffee table, where she had dropped it on her way upstairs, she went into the kitchen and placed it on the countertop, next to the coffee pot.

"He'll be sure and see it here. I would love to see the look on his face when he sees what's in this folder." She said. "I just know he will be lost without me to keep him in line. Well, he'll just have to get along without me. Because I am gone."

And with that she went to the garage, got in her car, opened the door, backed out, closed the garage door, and sped off down the street toward the city and her new life.

Standing on the corner Gabriel watched her drive past.

****

Saturday was the Mayor's morning to sleep in, which usually meant 7:00. But he didn't get back to sleep until almost 2:00 in the morning so he slept well past the hour. Helen finally came up from the kitchen to wake him.

"G.D., G. D. honey," Helen said as she shook his shoulder. "It's almost 8:00, are you gonna sleep all day?"

G.D. opened one eye. "Not a bad idea."

"Not a good idea, either. We have things to do today. Why are you so tired?"

"Had a bad dream last night. Actually it was more of a nightmare. Don't you remember me waking you up when I called out in my sleep?"

"No, I sure don't. Why don't you get up and come downstairs for some coffee and I'll make you breakfast."

"Okay, I'll be right down." G.D. said as he sat up on the edge of the bed.

Helen went back to the kitchen and was pouring herself a cup of coffee when the phone rang.

"Hello."

"Helen? This is Jayne. Is the Mayor there?"

"Good morning, Jayne. Yes. He's still upstairs. Wait a minute and I'll call him." Helen laid the phone down on the counter and went to the foot of the stairs. "G.D." she called. "Get the phone up there. It's Jayne. She wants to talk to you."

G. D. went to the table by the bed and picked up the phone. "Hi, Jayne, what's up?"

"I was just going by the Court House and there are a couple of people out in front with signs saying the Nativity Scene is unconstitutional."

"What? Who are they?"

"I think one of them is that Ira Freethinker guy from the triple A. And it looks like the other fellow is his partner Phil Faithless. Boy, there's a couple of names for you."

"What are they doing, picketing the Court House?"

"That's what it looks like."

"Don't they know its Saturday and there's nobody down there?"

"Evidently not. Shall I call the police?"

"No, they're not hurting anyone. I'll go down and talk to them after breakfast."

"Okay, Mr. Mayor. Just thought you ought to know."

"Right, thanks Jayne. Have a good weekend."

"You, too. So long."

"So long." G. D. hung up the phone and shook his head. "What a waste of time." He thought. "Picketing someplace that isn't even open. Well, they can just keep picketing until I've had my breakfast."

"What was that all about?" Helen asked as G. D. came into the kitchen.

"Jayne said she just drove by the Court House and there were a couple of guys out in front with signs."

"Pickets?"

"Seems so. Their signs said that the Nativity Scene is unconstitutional, or words to that effect."

"Did Jayne call the police?"

"No, I said not to bother, they weren't hurting anybody. I told her I'd go down and talk to them after breakfast."

"You know, G. D. this whole Nativity Scene thing is really getting out of hand. How can anything so innocent cause so much trouble?"

"I imagine that's what Herod thought when he heard about the birth of Jesus." G. D. said, laughing. "But it does seem to have a life of it's own. Even beyond Newton's Mill."

"Yes. The front page of the paper says that there will probably be TV and radio reporters at the City Council meeting on Tuesday."

"Oh no. Just what I needed. More pressure."

"G. D., you said you had a nightmare last night? Want to tell me about it?"

"Do you remember the old Ebenezer Scrooge story?"

"Sure, who doesn't? Every kid in school had to do a book report on it."

"Well, in my dream the ghost of Christmas Past..."

"The what?"

"I told you it was crazy. Anyway. The ghost of Christmas Past took me back to when we all used to gather at the Mill to sing carols on Christmas Eve."

"He took you?"

"In my dream, he did. I even saw old Colonel Newton, and Floyd Carver. And Archie, Hebert and you when we were kids. You were pretty cute, even then."

"Yeah, right. So, then what happened?"

"Next thing I knew another ghost shows up."

"The ghost of Christmas Present?"

"Yeah. He showed me how commercial everything has become. How they're taking Christ out of Christmas. It was eye opening."

"So I suppose the next ghost was Christmas Future?"

"That's the really scary part. There was no ghost of Christmas Future. Christmas Past said that if things don't change there won't be any Christmas anymore. That people will forget what it really means and why we celebrate it."

"And then?"

"That was when they told me that if there was no Christmas Future it was all my fault."

"All your fault?"

"Yes. They said that taking away the Nativity Scene was the start of forgetting Christmas. So it would be all my fault if I voted against it. That's when I woke up."

"I remember now. You sat up in bed and shouted something about it not being your fault."

"There was no getting back to sleep after that. So I went downstairs for some milk and a cookie or two."

"The age old cure for bad dreams." Helen laughed.

"That's when I found Gordon there, having milk and cookies."

"Did he have a bad dream, too?"

"No, but it seems he got into a little bit of trouble at school the other day."

"Oh?"

"Yes, seems he asked the teacher a question she couldn't answer."

"Uh oh."

G. D. went on to tell Helen about his talk with Gordon and reading the story of the Nativity that his Grandfather used to read at Christmas.

"That's what brought me downstairs after you left." Helen said. "I heard the two of you in the living room and when you began to read the story I came down quietly, and sat on the stairs to listen."

"It sure helped Gordon. And it opened my eyes to a thing or two as well. You know, I've been searching around for the answers to this whole problem. But I never looked in the right place."

"The right place?"

"Yes. I never asked God for help with it."

"Well, when we knelt to pray I was also asking Him for His help. To give you the right answer to the problem."

"The Bible says where two or more are gathered in His name there will He be also."

"So, did He give you the answer?"

"Not yet. But I sure feel a whole lot better knowing He's working on the problem with us."

****

"Ira, are you sure this is a good idea." Phil asked, through chattering teeth. "It's coldout here and there's nobody working at the Court House today. It's Saturday."

Ira and Phil had gone to the Newton Mill Press late Friday afternoon to discuss placing an ad in the paper prior to the Council meeting on Tuesday. Needless to say Mary Beth was less than enthusiastic about it and told them in no uncertain terms that it was her newspaper and she decided what went in it and what didn't and their ads sure weren't something she had any intention of running. So they could just take themselves out of her office. The only thing left for Ira and Phil to do was to picket the Court House. At least that's what Ira decided. So they went to a local sign shop to have the signs made up, and the owner turned them down. Two other shops did the same. So Ira and Phil went back to Ira's apartment and made the signs themselves.

"We have to get our message out to the people." Ira answered. "How else will they know that this whole Christmas thing is just a fairy tale?"

"Do you really believe that?" It was Gabriel. Neither of them had seen him come up to them.

"Oh, it's you." Ira sneered.

"Say, do you just appear out of nowhere?" Phil asked. "I didn't see you until you spoke."

"Oh, I was around. You were just too busy picketing to notice."

"So what do you want?" Ira snarled.

"Well, I overheard your conversation about Christmas just being a fairy tale."

"Yeah, so?"

"So, do you really believe that?"

"I sure do. There's no God. So if there's no God there can be no Jesus, and if there's no Jesus then there's no Christmas."

"What about you, Phil. I asked you once before if you believed there was no God. You sounded a little unsure of yourself when you answered."

Phil didn't want to answer these questions. They made him think. And thinking made his head hurt. It was easier just to go along with Ira. Agree with everything he said.

"Well?" Gabriel asked. "Are you positive that there is no God?"

"Why don't you leave him alone?" Ira said, as he stepped between Phil and Gabriel. "He believes the same things I believe. And I believe there is no God, so he believes there is no god. It's as simple as that."

"No, it's not as simple as that. Deciding whether there is a God or not is never simple. It goes against your nature. There is a longing inside each of you for God. He put it there. So if you decide there is no God then you deny the existence of a part of you. The part that counts."

"So that's why I feel like I do." Phil thought to himself. *"I'm missing a part of me that needs God."*

"There is no part like that in me." Ira stammered. " I know it."

"But there is in me." Phil spoke up. "I've been feeling like there was a part of me missing ever since I got involved with you and this crazy Atheist and Agnostics bunch."

"Phil, what are you saying?" Ira blurted out. "You're part of the group."

"Not anymore I'm not. It just dawned on me that everything you stand for is just lies. I can't be a part of this anymore. It's not right."

Phil handed his sign to Ira. "Here, take this. Now you have one for both hands. Makes you look twice as ignorant."

"Welcome back, Phil. Or should I call you Richard." Gabriel said, as they walked away.

****

Nathaniel Archibald was excited about the upcoming city council meeting. He had heard that there were going to be TV reporters and newspaper people from all over the state there to see how it all turned out. Archie wasn't so excited about the meeting. He was just excited about the possibility that someone from the TV station or the newspapers would want to interview him *"This could be a great opportunity for me to get better known outside of Newton's Mill."* He thought. *"A little TV exposure wouldn't hurt my political career at all."* Archie had long wanted to go farther as a politician than just being a city councilman. He would never run for Mayor, however. He had too much respect for G. D. to do that. And he was pretty sure he couldn't beat him, anyway. But he was looking toward to the fall when he might run for State Senator from his district. And this whole Nativity Scene controversy could be just the springboard he needs to get better known outside of the area.

"More coffee, dear?" Archie's wife Rebecca asked. "You seem deep in thought."

"Yes, thanks. I was just thinking about the city council meeting coming up. It could be a good opportunity for me."

"In what way?"

"The news last night said this Nativity Scene thing is getting exposure all across the country. Seems we're not the only city facing this kind of problem."

"I heard that. They said there will probably be TV and newspaper reporters at the meeting."

"Exactly. And what better way for me to get a little publicity and a boost for my campaign for State Senator next year."

"Oh, Nathan." Rebecca said. "Are you still thinking about running for state office?"

"Still thinking? I never stopped. I've gone as far as I can go here in Newton's Mill. If I want to go farther I've got to become better known. Get my name out. Let folks see me, hear me, find out what I stand for."

"What do you stand for?" Rebecca asked. She had an annoying habit of asking him questions he had no ready answer for.

"Well, I'm gonna have to work on that." Archie said. "But I'll come up with something before election time."

"Nathan, you know how I feel about you running for some state office that will take us out of Newton's Mill. This is our home. Why can't you just be content with being a city councilman, and running the paint store?" Archie had taken over his Dad's paint store when he passed away.

"We have a good life here. I'm not so sure if we moved to the capital that we would be happy."

"Rebecca, just think of the excitement of the political scene there. The parties. The meetings. The connections. Hanging out with the movers and the shakers. It's a whole new world, full of all sorts of possibilities."

Rebecca had heard this all before. Every election year Archie made noises that he wanted to run for a more prestigious office. And every year he managed to find some reason not to. But this year he seemed determined to make the run. The sad thing about it was, Archie would never be able to convince enough people that there was any substance behind his long-winded speeches. She knew that most folks felt Archie was just a windbag.

"Well," she said. "I'm not so sure this Nativity Scene thing is gonna give you the kind of exposure you want."

"Why not? I voted in favor of it, didn't I?"

"Yes. But what if G.D. votes against it? And he could, you know. Then you would be on the losing side. That wouldn't do much for your campaign."

Archie sat quietly for a minute. "I hadn't thought about that." He said. "You don't suppose G. D. could possibly vote against it, do you?"

"I'm really not sure. I've heard that he's under a lot of pressure from all sides on this. So, he could decide to vote either way."

Archie saw his political future fading away before his eyes. If the Mayor voted against the Nativity Scene that would be the end of it for his run for State Senator. Being on the losing side of anything wasn't a plus for a political campaign. He had to talk to G.D. and convince him to vote in favor of the Nativity. He pushed his chair back from the table and stood up.

"Where are you going, Nathan? It's Saturday, and I have things for you to do around the house here."

"No time for that. I've got to find the Mayor and make sure he votes the right way."

"The right way for who?"

"Why, the right way for me, of course.

****

Cora Nickels was hoping she might run into this Gabriel fellow she had heard about. He seemed to be someone she would be interested in talking to. But right now she was too busy.

"It's a shame what J. B. pays these Santas." She said to herself. *"As hard as he expects them to work I'm surprised anyone would want to do it. I just hope that this little salary increase will slip right by J. B. He doesn't pay too much attention to salaries. Just profits. And maybe Finster will be able to get back a couple of those that quit so the others won't have to work so hard."*

Cora was almost the exact opposite of J.B. Many folks couldn't understand how she could put up with him. But Cora knew something most folks didn't. J. B. had a soft side that he wouldn't admit to. He preferred to have people think of him as a hardheaded businessman. That's why he and Cora got along so well. And she knew just how to get around his stubbornness to get what she wanted. And right now she was just finishing up entering the new salary structure into the computer when J.B. walked in.

"Cora, have you seen the sales figures for the last quarter?" He asked.

"There right here, Dear." Cora handed him a stack of papers. "They look pretty good this early in the Christmas Season. We might have a good year after all."

J. B. sat down in a chair in front of Cora's desk.

"What is it, J. B.?" Cora could see he had something on his mind.

"I was just thinking about what that fellow Gabriel said the other day. I'm still not sure I know what he meant."

"You mean when he said you couldn't take it with you?"

"Yes. I mean, I'm not planning on going anywhere."

"I don't think that's what he meant." Cora sat back in her chair and looked at J.B.

"I'm pretty sure you're right. It seemed to have a deeper meaning than that. And it's really got me thinking."

"About what?"

"About not being able to take it with me. If I can't, and I know that's true, then what am I doing working so hard here? Making all this money. What good is it?"

"Well, it gives us a good life." Cora wasn't sure just how to answer these questions. She knew what the answers were for her. But they might not be the right answers for J. B.

"That's not what I mean." J. B. sat silently for a moment. "Cora, I've spent my whole life making money. It's been the main goal in my life. But that simple statement from that fellow Gabriel has made me take a good long look at myself. And I didn't like what I saw. I've, we've, got plenty of money. More than we need in Newton's Mill."

"What are you trying to say, J.B.?"

"I'm trying to say that I'm tired of being J.B. Nickels, the money hungry business man. I don't know what's come over me. All I know is the money hasn't made me happy.

Oh, don't get me wrong. I'm happy with you, and our life together has been wonderful. But there's got to be more than that."

"There is." Cora answered.

"What? Help me out here, honey. I'm struggling. I've never felt like this before."

"You know, J. B. all these years we've been married I've been taking care of the financial end of the business. I keep the books, pay the salaries, and keep track of the inventory. Everything it takes to keep us making money. But there's something else I do, too."

"Something else?"

"Yes, I set aside some of the money we make to help others that need it. The homeless shelter, the Women's shelter, most of the charities here in Newton's Mill and the Newton Mill hospital have all been places that we have supported all these years."

"I never knew."

"Right. Because as long as the bottom line showed black everything was fine. And I made sure that it did. So, whether you knew it or not a lot of the money we made was going to help others. But, I always gave the money anonymously, so the word would not get back to you."

"That's sort of sneaky, you know." J.B. smiled. "But it certainly is something I know you would do."

"Listen, dear, if you really want to make a difference I can think of many more ways to use all this money we're making. There are a lot of needs out there."

"What do you suggest?"

"Oh, J. B., I've got a thousand suggestions just waiting to be tended to." Cora's excitement got the better of her and she went to J. B. and threw her arms around him.

J. B. held her for a long while. It had been some time since they had held each other like this. He liked it, a lot.

"You know the first thing I want to do?" J.B. whispered in her ear.

"What's that?"

"I need to give the Santas a raise. They deserve it for putting up with me."

Cora smiled over his shoulder and held him tighter.

****

G.D. parked his car in the lot next to the Court House. He saw Ira walking back and forth in front of the building holding a sign. And there was another sign stuck in the ground at the side of the steps leading up to the front door. *"I thought Jayne said there were two of them."* He thought. *"Well, it's pretty cold out here, maybe the other one went for something warm to drink."* He got out of his car and walked over to where Ira stood, shivering in the cold.

"Hello, Ira." G. D. greeted him. "What's up?"

"I'm just exercising my constitutional right of protest."

"That's nice. What are you protesting?"

"The Nativity Scene and its illegal placement on government property."

"My secretary said there were two of you."

"There were. But my ex-associate lost the strength of his

convictions and left."

"He lost what?"

"The strength of his convictions. That fellow Gabriel messed with his mind and he decided he wasn't really an Atheist."

"Gabriel, eh? Well, I'm not surprised. He can be a pretty convincing fellow at times. But let's get back to this picketing. Don't you know City Hall is closed? It's Saturday. Almost no one works on Saturday down here."

"That's not important. What is important is that the people of Newton's Mill realize that the Nativity Scene is just a fairy tale about something that never happened. There wasn't any Jesus, so there can't be any Nativity Scene. No Jesus, no Nativity. It's as simple as that."

"Not so simple. There's probably more historical evidence of the life of Jesus than there is of you. It's a promise that's over 2000 years old."

"What promise?"

"The promise of a Savior. Someone to save us from our sins."

"Baloney. I don't need no Savior to save me from my sins."

"Ira, I know a lot of people that could use saving from their sins, myself included. But of all the people I know, you're probably the one most likely to need it."

"Well, I don't believe in God, and if I don't believe in God, then I don't believe in sin, either."

"What do you believe in, Ira?" The Mayor asked.

Now here was a question that Ira wasn't expecting. It was easy to tell everyone what he didn't believe in. But he never really thought about what he did believe in. And he didn't know how to answer.

"Well?" G. D. said, after a few seconds. "Got an answer for that question?"

"I, uh, I..." Ira was stumped. It was getting a little uncomfortable here right now. But he couldn't figure out a good way to answer, or a good way to change the subject. He began to sweat, even in the cold weather. Ira had never bothered to take a good look at what he believed. So he realized that he didn't believe in anything.

"I believe...I believe... I believe it's too cold to stand out here and argue with you. I'm leaving." Ira turned and started to walk away.

"Hey, Ira."

"Yes?" Ira turned.

"You forgot your other sign."

****

Archie was driving past the Court House when he noticed G. D. standing at the bottom of the steps watching someone walking away carrying two crudely lettered signs. *"That looks like that Ira Freethinker from that bunch of Atheists."* Archie thought. *"I wonder what he was doing at the Court House?"*

Archie pulled over to the curb and rolled down his window. "Hey, Mr. Mayor. What are you doing down here on a Saturday?" He shouted.

"Hey, Archie." G. D. shouted back. "Just taking care of some business. What's up?"

"I need to talk to you for a minute."

"Okay, pull into the lot and keep the heater running. I'm freezing."

Archie parked the car next to the mayor's car and G. D. got in. "Whew, it's really getting colder out there. Nice in here, though."

"Was that Ira Freethinker I saw walking away when I came up?"

"Yes, that was him."

"What was he doing?"

"Well, believe it or not he was picketing the Court House."

"On Saturday?" Doesn't he know nobody works down here on

Saturday?"

"That's what I asked him. He said he was exercising his constitutional right of protest."

"His what?"

"Never mind. He's just confused about what he does, or doesn't believe. What did you want to talk to me about?"

"I understand that there will be some TV and newspaper coverage of the meeting on Tuesday."

"That's what I hear. I'm not looking forward to it." "But it could mean some national exposure for Newton's Mill. Put us on the map, so to speak."

"Could mean a circus, too. I don't know why this is turning into such a big deal."

"Because it's a problem everywhere. Just look in the papers, G. D. It's like a crusade to get rid of Christmas."

"Yeah, you're right there. My boy Gordon got in trouble the other day for asking the teacher

why they couldn't mention anything about Christmas anymore."

"Really? What did she say?"

"Couldn't answer. Sent him to the principal's office. He asked him the same question."

"And?"

"He couldn't answer either."

"You see what I mean?"

"Yes. And all this stuff is really putting the pressure on me for Tuesday night."

"Ah, yes. Tuesday night." Archie said. 'That's just what I want to talk to you about."

"Oh no," G. D. thought. *"Here it comes."*

" This may seem somewhat selfish of me but you know how I've toyed with the idea of running for State Senator?"

"I do. But what has that got to do with this?"

"Well, I'm hoping that with all the attention we're getting it might be a chance for me to become a little better known outside of Newton's Mill."

"How do figure that?"

"Well, if I get the chance to talk to one of the reporters or newscasters I could get my name out there which would help me in my campaign."

"I see. But what has that got to do with me?"

"This morning I was discussing this situation with Rebecca and how advantageous it would be for me to be on the winning side in this conflict."

"The winning side?"

"Yes. You know I voted for the placement of the Nativity on the Court House lawn?"

"Yes, eventually."

"Well, Rebecca said that there was a chance you might vote against it because you're under a lot of pressure and then that would mean I would be on the losing side and that wouldn't be very good for my campaign." Archie said, all in one breath.

"Slow down, Arch. Take a breath, your face is turning red. Now, as much as I would like to help you score some points for your campaign I haven't made up my mind yet just how I'm going to vote. So you will have to wait until Tuesday to find out."

"Could you just give me a hint as to how you are leaning?"

"Not even a hint. But for your information I'm not leaning one way or the other right now. So it could go your way, or not."
"Surely you're not going to vote against it? Why, it's a tradition here. You'll disappoint a lot of people, including myself."

"I'm sure. But I need to consider all the arguments for and against."

Archie sat for a moment. He couldn't very well argue with G.

D. over this. They had been friends for far to long. And, deep in his heart he knew that G. D. would make the right decision, what ever that was.

"I'm sorry, G. D. Sometimes I let my ambition get in the way. I shouldn't be putting this kind of pressure on you. I know you'll make the right decision for Newton's Mill."

"Thanks, Archie. You know you're one of my closest friends, and I would do anything for you. But I'm still undecided about this whole thing. You'll just have to wait until Tuesday night. But good luck with dealing with the TV and newspaper people. They can be a ruthless bunch sometimes." G. D. got out of the car.

"I understand. I'll be praying for you. And I'm glad it's not me." Archie laughed.

"Thanks a lot, Archie. The prayers would be appreciated." He shut the door and stood watching as Archie pulled out of the parking lot and headed back toward his house.

"And I wish it wasn't me, too." G. D. thought.

****

It had been a good day at the bookstore. People were beginning to get serious about their Christmas buying and so they kept Hebert and Katie busy most of the day. The two of them worked well together and, not unexpectedly, Paul came in to take Katie to lunch and wound up pitching in to help. When things slowed down a bit Hebert pushed the two young people out the door to go for lunch. They reluctantly agreed but only after promising to let them bring him a sandwich.

Alone in the bookstore Hebert found himself thinking about Bertha. She had been gone longer now than ever and didn't even bother to call last night. *"I wonder just what's going on with her."* He thought. *"I know she's not happy. Hasn't been happy for a long time. But I don't know what to do about it. Maybe we should sit down and try and talk it out. Yes, that's a good idea. As soon as she gets home we will have to talk this out."*

"Hello, Mr. Humble." It was Gabriel.

"Gabriel." Hebert jumped. He hadn't heard him come in.

"Sorry, didn't mean to startle you." "Oh, that's okay. I am just used to hearing the buzzer on the door sound when someone comes in. I must have missed it."

"Well, you did seem deep in thought." Gabriel answered. "Anything wrong?"

"No," Hebert hesitated. "No, just thinking about something I have to do this evening."

"Something fun, I hope."

"I'm not so sure it will be fun. But it is necessary."

"Oh."

"I'm sorry, Gabriel. Can I help you find something?"

"Actually I'm just browsing. I love book stores."

"So do I. That's why I have such an enjoyable time operating this one."

"It must be satisfying to be able to help someone find just the book they are looking for."

"Or, help them discover a book that they might have overlooked."

"How long have you owned the bookstore?" Gabriel asked.

"Gosh, let's see. I bought it just a short while after Bertha and I were married."

"Does Bertha enjoy the bookstore as much as you do?"

"She's never set foot in it." Hebert said softly.

"Never?"

"Nope. She thinks it's just a little nothing bookstore that will never amount to anything."

"Her words?"

"Exactly. She put up the money for me to buy it. To give me something to do and keep me out of the way, I guess. But it has been a bright spot in my life."

"She put up the money?"

"Yes. Her family had a great deal of money, which she inherited when they passed on. And she has never let me forget that it was her money that bought it."

"Hebert, I sense that things are not too happy around your household."

"It shows that much, does it?"

"To me it does. But I'm sometimes more aware of things than others."

"Well, that's part of what I have to do this evening."

"And that is?"

"I have decided that Bertha and I need to sit down and try to figure out what we need to do to make our marriage work."

"That's important. But, what if she won't discuss it."

"I'm hoping that her being away for a few days will have softened her attitude."

"I hope you're right, Hebert. But remember what I said to you the last time we talked."

"Yes, that things would get better for me, soon. But I still don't know what you mean by that."

"You will. You will. I better be going now. I'm sure Katie and Paul will be back soon with your lunch."

"You know, Gabriel. Talking to you can sure be confusing."

"Yes, it can, can't it?" Gabriel laughed.

This time when he went out the door the buzzer sounded.

****

Paul and Katie got their sandwiches and took a table by the window where they could have a good view of the shoppers in the Mall.

"I just love to watch people." Katie said.

"And I just love to watch you." Paul thought. "We have sure been busy at the store today. I guess people are getting serious about Christmas Shopping." Katie added.

"You and Mr. H. work really well together. I think you are both very suited for the work you do." Paul said. "It's fun for me just to help out and watch you two at work. You are so helpful to everyone that comes in the store. No wonder its such a busy place."

"Well, Mr. H. loves books. And he loves helping folks find just what they are looking for. And I've really learned a lot since I started working there."

"He was fun at the game last night, too."

"I know. I never knew he could be so much fun."

"Yes, what a surprise."

"Not if you ask my Mom."

"What?"

"She says that Mr. H. used to be one of the funniest guys in school when they were kids."

"Really? What happened?"

"I guess Bertha happened. Mom says she just took over every part of his life. It got so bad he couldn't even hang out with any of his friends."

"Wow. That's too bad."

"You know, I think he isn't very happy at home." Katie said between bites of her sandwich.

"Why do you say that?"

"Well, when he first comes in the store in the morning he is very quiet and hardly smiles at all. It usually takes him about an hour to loosen up."

"He seemed fine this morning."

"That's probably because Bertha has been out of town for several days."

Paul sat quietly for a minute or two, watching the crowds outside the window. "That's not how a marriage should be." He said softly.

"What?"

"I said that's not how a marriage should be. A marriage should be full of love, and laughter and happiness, even when the times are tough. That's the way I want our marriage to be."

"WHAT?" Katie blurted out.

"Oops." Paul turned beet red.

"Did you say that's how you want our marriage to be?"

"Uh, well, yes." Paul stammered.

"Is this a proposal?" Katie asked softly.

"It might be."

"Well, if it is, I accept." Katie said as she threw her arms around Paul and gave him a big kiss.

"Katie," Paul pulled away from the kiss. "People are staring."

"I don't care, Paul Moore. I've been waiting for years for you to ask me to marry you." Katie shouted. Causing even more heads to turn.

"Years?" Paul asked, growing even redder by the second.

"Ever since the third grade, when you tripped over my foot and fell flat on your face."

"I don't remember that."

"Well, I do. I've loved you ever since."

"So, I guess we're engaged?" Paul said, wiping the lipstick off his face.

"You better believe it, buster. I'm not letting you get away."

By this time everyone in the sandwich shop was laughing and applauding, thoroughly enjoying the show.

"This wasn't exactly the way I had dreamed of asking you to marry me."

"Are you kidding? It was great. Wait until I tell Mr. H. and my Mom. Oh, and I'm sure Jim will get a big kick out of it."

"I'll never hear the end of it." Paul groaned.

****

On some days, when Cora took lunch she would sit on a bench in the concourse of the mall and watch the crowds while she ate.

After her morning conversation with J. B. she was even more determined to find this Gabriel fellow and talk with him. So she hoped that she might find him in the crowds.

"I don't even know what he looks like." She thought. *"So I don't know how I expect to find him in all these people."*

"Hi, Mrs. Nickels." It was Finster.. "Checking out the crowds?"

"Oh, hello, Alan. Yes, I like to watch the people. Some of them are so, so, interesting."

"Interesting is one word I might use. I can think of a couple of others, too. How is your morning going?" Finster sat down next to her.

"Better than you might imagine. In fact, it has been a most surprising morning. Yes, a most surprising morning."

"How so?"

"You know this fellow Gabriel that you told me about?"

"Uh huh."

"Well, it seems that he had a talk with my husband a day or so ago."

"And?"

"It made very big impression on J.B."

"Is that good or bad?"

"In this case it's good. Very good." Cora went on to tell Alan about her conversation of the morning with J.B. As she talked she could see the look of disbelief in Alan's eyes. *"I guess if I hadn't been there I wouldn't believe this story, either."* She thought.

"That's amazing Mrs. Nickels." Alan said when she had finished. "And unbelievable."

"And the best part is that he suggested we raise the salaries of the Santas because he expects a lot out of them."

"What?"

"Yes, it was his idea. I didn't have the heart to tell him I had already done it." Cora smiled.

"And all of this just because he talked with Gabriel?"

"It would seem so."

"Just what did Gabriel say to him?"

"That he couldn't take it with him."

"He couldn't take what with him?"

"Anything. I would never have expected just a simple sentence like that could work such a change in J.B."

"This Gabriel guy seems to have that affect on folks. Just this morning I was talking with Rufus Pettifogger."

"The OARD Pettifogger."

"The same one. Only he's not with the OARD anymore."

"He's not?"

"No, it seems he had a talk with Gabriel that got him to thinking, too. He decided that he really wasn't suited to be a part of that organization."

"Now that is interesting." Cora answered. "I would love to talk with this Gabriel myself."

"I just saw him come out of Humble's Book Store. Wait here, I'll see if I can find him." Alan got up and worked his way into the crowd. "Excuse me, Mrs. Nickels. May I join you?"

"I'm sorry. Do I know you?" Cora asked of the tall man who sat down beside her.

"My name is Gabriel. And I hear you have been looking for me."

"My, that was fast."

"What?"

"I said that was fast. Alan just left a moment ago to find you."

"And here I am." Gabriel said, laughing. "What can I do for

you?"

"Believe it or not, you have already done it."

"I have?"

"Yes, your conversation with my husband made a profound impression on him. I would say it has actually changed his life, and mine."

"For the better, I hope."

"Most definitely. So I owe you a great big thank you."

"You're welcome, I think. Can you tell me in just what way your husband has changed?"

"Gladly. Since you played such a large part in it." Cora told Gabriel all that had taken place that morning and how she was amazed at the change in her husband.

"You know, Mrs. Nickels," Gabriel said when she had finished. "I wouldn't be too surprised at the change in your husband. He's always been a good man. He just let money and success get in his way."

"I know. And I tried to tell him but he never seemed to get the message."

"Sometimes it isn't so much the message," Gabriel said as he stood up and turned to leave. "As it is the messenger."

****

"Mr. H., Mr. H." Katie shouted, as she burst through the door of the bookstore. "You will never in a million years guess what just happened."

Hebert couldn't remember ever seeing Katie so excited. "Calm down, Katie. You'll have a stroke." He said, joining in her laughter. "Now what is this big momentous thing that just happened?"

Katie stopped for a moment to get her breath and Hebert saw Paul, looking embarrassed, just coming into the store behind her. *"I'll bet this has something to do with Paul."* He thought. *"And it must be something big to get Katie so excited."*

"Okay, Mr. H., okay. I've got my breath back."

"Good, now what is so exciting?"

"Are you ready for this? Maybe you better sit down."

"From the look on Paul's face I think maybe he better sit down." Hebert said, laughing.

"Paul asked me to marry him!"

"He what?" Hebert couldn't believe his ears. "So that's why

Paul looks so uncomfortable."

"Yes. He asked me to marry him. Well, I mean, it was kind of unexpected."

"Kind of is right." Paul said.

"Actually, I think it just slipped out. But I accepted before he could change his mind. Isn't that great?"

"Katie, I'm so happy for you. And for you, too, Paul."

"Thanks Mr. Humble," Paul said. "This wasn't exactly the way I wanted to do it but, well, the result is the same. So I guess we're engaged."

"You guess?" Katie laughed. "You're doggone right we're engaged." And she threw her arms around him and gave him a big kiss again.

"Alright, you two." Hebert interrupted. "Unwrap yourself from around that young man's neck and the two of you get out of here. You need to go tell your Mother, Katie. And I suppose you better let your folks know as well, Paul."

"Right, Mr. H." Katie said, letting go of Paul. "But what about the store?"

"I can handle this store without you for an event as big as this. Now go."

Katie gave Hebert a big hug and grabbed Paul by the hand and the two of them ran out the door.

"Be careful you don't knock somebody down." He shouted after them but they were gone into the crowd.

"Now that's the way love should be," He thought. *"That's the way love should be."*

****

"So, G. D." Helen said as he came through the door. "Did you get those picketers straightened out down at the Court House?"

"Well, there was only one there when I arrived."

"What happened to the other one?"

"Seems he lost the strength of his convictions."

"What's that mean?"

"It means he had a conversation with that Gabriel fellow and decided he wasn't an Atheist or an Agnostic after all."

"So, who was there?"

"It was Ira Freethinker, of course. But, you know, I asked him a question and he didn't have an answer. Made some lame excuse about it being too cold to stand outside and argue, picked up his signs and left."

"So, what question did you ask him that he couldn't answer?"

"He was all wound up telling me what he didn't believe in so I just asked him what he did believe in."

"Stumped him?"

"Big time. I really don't think he ever stopped to ask himself that question."

"Well, it seems like maybe it's easier for some folks to shout about what they don't believe in, than to talk about what they do."

"At least it's easier for Ira. Oh, and just as Ira was leaving Archie drove up."

"Looking for you?"

"Right. Wanted to talk about the meeting on Tuesday. He's excited that there will be TV and newspaper reporters there and wanted to suggest that I vote for the Nativity display since it wouldn't be good for his political aspirations if he was on the losing side of this argument."

"So, I suppose he's thinking about running for State Senator again. That should make Rebecca ecstatic. I know she hates it when he starts talking about running for anything that might take them out of Newton's Mill. But what did he mean about being on the losing side of the argument?"

"He voted for the Nativity. He's concerned that if I vote against it he looks like he supported a losing cause."

"That's sounds like Archie."

"I convinced him that I still hadn't made up my mind which way I was going to vote."

"G.D., I'm getting very concerned about this whole voting thing. I know it's got you under a lot of pressure."

"Yeah, even gives me nightmares thinking about it. And the worst part about it is that I just don't have any clear indication of what's right."

"Should you talk with Artemis? Get some more perspective on it?"

"I thought about that. Maybe I'll see if I can get a few minutes with him after church. It might help."

"Are you interested in my thoughts?"

"Certainly."

"The Nativity Scene has been around for as long as any of us can remember. But over the years it's just sort of become a thing."

"A thing? What do mean."

"Well, we don't all gather together in front of it on Christmas Eve to sing carols and fellowship with folks anymore."

"I know, and I miss that."

"I miss it, too. But I'm not sure that voting to keep it there for Christmas will make any difference in that."

"You might be right. Seems folks are just too busy doing last minute Christmas shopping, wrapping presents and getting ready for the Christmas Dinner to show up down there. It just sort of faded away."

"Does that mean Christmas is fading away, too."

" I sometimes think the meaning of it is getting harder and harder to remember. Everything is holiday this, and holiday that, and you can't sing Christmas carols anymore if they mention Christ because it might offend someone who doesn't celebrate the birth of Jesus is getting to be more than I can stand. I love Christmas. I love what it stands for. But lately I feel like I'm in the minority."

"And that just makes this decision all the harder, doesn't it?" Helen asked. "Because what may be right for you might not necessarily be what's right for all the people of Newton's Mill?"

"There are so many new people here in our town now." G. D. answered. "People who don't know, or care about the traditions we had when we were still just a small mill town. But they're part of our town now. Part of the people I represent as Mayor. So I have to consider them in whatever decision I make."

"You know that whatever decision you make, there will be people who don't agree with it?"

"It's always that way. But somehow this decision seems bigger, and more important than any of the others."

"In what way?"

"It's sort of like one of those guys from my dream said. If I vote against it it's another step on the road to making Christmas a forgotten celebration."

"Oh, G. D., you don't believe that, do you?"

"I don't know, Helen. I just know I would hate to have Newton's Mill become the town that forgot Christmas."

****

It had been an exciting day at Hebert's book store. The news about Katie and Paul was the topper to a day that saw an increase in sales. At times it seemed there were more people than the store could hold. And when he finally closed the doors and counted the receipts for the day it turned out to be the best sales day the store had ever had. So, he was pretty happy when he pulled his car into the driveway and went into the house.

"Bertha." He called. "I'm home." But there was no answer. "That's odd. I would have expected her to be home by this time."

Hebert went up the stairs and checked Bertha's bedroom.

Something didn't look right. The covers on the bed were disturbed, as though something, or someone had been sitting there. Then he noticed that the door to her closet was open. He switched on the light and saw that the closet was empty.

"What's going on here?" He thought. "Where are her clothes?"

Looking around the bedroom it seemed that nothing else was missing. But, because Bertha's bedroom was strictly her domain he couldn't be sure. She seldom allowed him to come in there.

He switched off the closet light and stood quietly at the foot of the bed, slowly coming to the conclusion that she was gone. He was a little surprised at his response. He was almost relieved.

"What's the matter with me?" He thought. *"I should be feeling a loss. Or anger, or confusion. But all I feel is relieved. Have I been that unhappy all these years?"*

He left the bedroom and went down the stairs to the kitchen. Turning on the light he immediately noticed the large brown envelope by the coffee maker. He picked it up and sat down at the kitchen table. He looked at it a long time before opening it. Lifting the flap he pulled out a stack of legal looking papers, and a note in Bertha's handwriting. It was a short note.

"Hebert," Bertha had written. "Inside this envelope are all the papers necessary to complete the steps I have taken to extricate myself from our marriage, our house, and the miserable little town of Newton's Mill. I have generously allowed you to keep that silly little bookstore you love so much, and when you have sold our house, which should bring a sizable amount of money, you may keep one half. I will expect you to review the documents enclosed herein, take the necessary steps to complete them and forward them to the legal firm of Carpenter and Fitch. Their card is attached to the forms. I desire to have no further contact with you, or anyone else from Newton's Mill. I feel I have been generous, far beyond any obligation you may feel I owe you. Therefore I will expect you to expedite this matter so we can both get on with our lives."

"She didn't even sign her name to the bottom." Hebert noted. "All these years I knew she wasn't happy here, but I never expected this." He sat at the table going through the documents that Bertha had prepared. She had been very thorough. Everything was pretty much in order just as she said in her note.

Hebert set the papers down on the table, got up and went to the stove. He put on a pot of water for tea, got a cup out of the cabinet and a tea bag from the canister on the countertop. He needed to do these simple things to get his mind around all that had just happened. When the water was hot he poured it into the cup and placed the pot back on the stove. He sat back down at the table with his tea and took another look at Bertha's note. This time, when he read it, a thought began to form in his mind.

"I guess I'm free." He said, and was surprised at the thought.

****

The phone rang as G. D. was finishing up some paper work that he had brought home on Friday.

"Hello." He said.

"G. D., it's Hebert. Have you got a minute to talk?"

"Sure, Hebert. What's up?"

"Bertha's left me."

"What?"

"I said Bertha's left me."

"How do you know?"

"When I got home from the store today she wasn't in the house. And neither were her clothes."

"That's strange."

"Maybe not so strange. She also left me a packet of papers and a note."

"Want to tell me what the note said."

"Yeah, that's why I called." Hebert read the note to G. D. and then filled him in on all the documents that were with it."

"Sounds like she was pretty thorough, Hebert. Did you have any idea?"

"Well, I was a little concerned that she was away in the city for so long. She never usually goes for more than a day. But, she was pretty upset when she left so I just figured she was taking longer to get settled down."

"Looks like she was spending her time doing something else."

"Obviously. The reason I called G. D. was to set up a time for you to take a look at all the documents and make sure they're legal and all."

"I'd be happy to. Why don't you come by the Court House on Monday morning and I'll take a look at them for you."

"Okay. What time would be good?"

"How about nine?"

"Sounds good. I'll get Katie to mind the store while I'm gone. Oh, by the way. Here's a little news on a happier note. It seems Paul finally got around to asking Katie to marry him."

"Are you serious? I thought he would never get up the nerve."

"Well, actually, it seems it just sort of slipped out and Katie accepted before he had a chance to change his mind."

"That Katie is one sharp girl." G. D. laughed.

"I'm very happy for the both of them."

"Hebert? How are you holding up with all this Bertha mess?"

"Maybe it's cruel of me to say so, but I feel sort of relieved. Life with Bertha has not been easy. But I took her for better or for worse, and so I just figured this was the worse part. But, you know something strange?"

"What's that?"

"I have had a couple of conversations with that fellow Gabriel that's new in town, and he told me that things were going to get better for me soon. Do you suppose this is what he meant?'

"Hebert, talking with Gabriel can sometimes be very interesting."

"That's putting it mildly. He seems to know an awful lot about Newton's Mill and the folks that live here."

"I've noticed that, too. It's a little spooky, when you come to think of it."

"Well, I don't want to take up any more of your time. I'll see you Monday morning."

"Looking forward to it. Goodnight, Hebert."

"Goodnight, G.D. and thanks for being such a good friend."

G.D. hung up the phone just as Helen came in from the kitchen.

"Who was that on the phone?" She asked.

"It was Hebert. And you'll never guess why he called."

"To talk about the Nativity Scene?"

"Nope. Seems Bertha has left him."

"What?"

"That was my reaction as well. She evidently came back from the city while he was at work, cleaned out her closet and left him a packet of legal documents terminating their marriage, putting the house up for sale, and generally putting an end to her presence in his life and in Newton's Mill."

"What about the bookstore?"

"Seems she left him that. Called it a 'silly little bookstore'."

"That's shocking news. How is he holding up?"

"Now, that's the interesting part. He says he feels relieved."

"G.D., that's not so interesting. How many years has that poor man put up with Bertha and her overbearing, pushy ways? She has made his life miserable since that day in school when she decided to take over his life. Maybe this sounds cruel, but I'm happy for him. Hebert was always such a gentle person, with a great sense of humor. And Bertha just crushed all that. Maybe now he can get back to being the old Hebert. No, I'm not sorry she's gone."

"I guess I feel pretty much the same way. It's always been sort of painful to see how she ran his life. He's coming to the office on Monday to have me look at the papers she left him. Wants to make sure everything is on the up and up."

"That's probably pretty smart. I'm afraid I wouldn't trust Bertha in this matter at all."

"Something else he told me. A little better news."

"And that would be?"

"I guess Paul finally got around to asking Katie to marry him."

"Are you serious?"

"Hebert said that Paul sort of let it slip and Katie accepted before he had a chance to change his mind."

"Smart girl."

"Very. Well, I guess we should head up to bed. I'm looking forward to Artemis' sermon tomorrow. Something tells me it's gonna be a good one."

****

Sunday

The Reverend Artemis Brown sat quietly to the left of the pulpit, listening to the choir as it wrapped up the music of the morning. Artemis always used this time to gather his thoughts and get ready to present his sermon. But this morning he found himself scanning the faces in the pews in front of him. There was the Mayor and his wife, in their usual spot, and Katie Black and her mother sitting close to the front. Something was different there, though. Sitting next to Katie was Paul Moore. Artemis knew Paul was sweet on Katie but this was the first time they had sat together in church. And there was a big smile on Katie's face as she and Paul sat shoulder to shoulder. *"I'll have to find out what's going on there."* He thought to himself, and smiled. *"I'll bet there's good news to be heard."*

As he scanned the rest of the congregation his eyes were drawn to a familiar face, but not one he had ever seen in his church before. "Rufus Pettifogger?" Now what's he doing here?" He asked himself. Then he noticed that Rufus was sitting next to Gabriel. *"I wonder if Gabriel has any thing to do with this?"* And then sitting next to Gabriel was that Atheist fellow Phil Faithless. Now Artemis was really intrigued. This Gabriel fellow seemed to have some strange friends.

The choir finished and Deacon Corliss got up to make the

announcements and take the offering. While this was going on Artemis took another look at his sermon for the morning. He had some important things to say, especially in light of the controversy that was surrounding the Nativity Scene. When the announcements were made and the offering taken Deacon Corliss returned to his seat. Artemis stood and walked slowly to the pulpit.

****

Rufus Pettifogger hadn't been in a church in years. He had come at the invitation of Gabriel and was surprised to find Phil Faithless there also. The three of them sat near the back of the church, with Gabriel in the middle. Rufus had done a lot of thinking over the past couple of days and when he made his decision to abandon the OARD he found Gabriel, or rather, it seemed Gabriel found him, to tell him about it. *"Somehow,"* He thought at the time. *"This Gabriel seems to be in the right spot at the right time. I wonder how he does it?"* "I'm overjoyed at your decision." Gabriel told him. "I knew that you were not the sort of person that could represent an organization like the OARD. You just had to realize it yourself."

"I will tell you, Gabriel, I feel as though a great weight were lifted off my shoulders."

"Of course you do. It's the weight of knowing you were doing the wrong thing. That's something you won't have to worry about anymore."

"And that feels good, too."

"Say, Rufus, I'm going over to Pastor Brown's church in the morning. I hear he's got a great sermon ready. Would you like to go with me?"

"Uh, well, I haven't been in a church in, well, in a long time. Not since I was a kid, actually."

"That's okay. I'm sure the church roof won't fall in." Gabriel laughed. "Why don't I stop by your apartment in the morning. We can walk over together."

"I guess so. See you then."

"Oh, there will be someone else going with us. A fellow named Richard Foster."

"Is he new in town? I don't recognize the name."

"Oh, he's been around awhile. But he used to call himself Phil."

"Used to call himself Phil?"

"Yes, Phil. Phil Faithless."

"The Atheist and Agnostics guy?"

"The very same."

"But I thought he didn't believe in God."

"He thought he didn't, too. Guess he changed his mind."

"After talking to you, I'll bet."

"Yep. See you in the morning."

****

G.D. had sat quietly during the first part of the service. His mind was still going back and forth over the Nativity Scene problem. But when Artemis got up to speak he gave him his full attention. *"I hope something in the sermon this morning will give me a clue as to what I'm supposed to do about this whole situation."* He thought.

"Good morning, friends." Artemis began, and then waited while the congregation returned his greeting. "My sermon this morning will be a little shorter than usual. Do I hear an amen?"

Several in the congregation called out an amen, while the rest just laughed. "But just because it's shorter doesn't make it any less important. Especially in light of the world today." Artemis paused and surveyed the crowd. "As I look around this church I see the faces of old friends. People who have lived here in Newton's Mill most all of their lives. And I also see some faces that have only recently been coming to our church. And, there is a face or two out there that have surprised me with their attendance this morning." Some in the congregation chuckled.

"But I welcome them. All are welcome here in God's house. That's the wonderful thing about God. He welcomes anyone into his house. His doors are always open. But have you ever wondered just why God welcomes us? Sinners one and all? Why does His mercy fall so freely on us? We certainly don't deserve it.

"I want to call your attention to a verse of scripture. It's one I'm sure most of you learned in Sunday School, and I'm pretty sure almost everyone here is familiar with it. It's John 3:16. Why don't you all say it along with me."

On the two screens to either side of the platform the words to the verse flashed up. The congregation joined Artemis as he read.

"For God so loved the world that He gave His one and only Son, that whoever believes in Him shall not perish but have eternal life."

There were several amens from the congregation when they had finished.

"There's the reason, folks. Because He loved the world. That's you, and me, and the Mayor, and Councilman Archibald, and even J.B. Nickels. He loves us all. And He sent us the gift of His Son to show us that love. So, what did the world do with that gift?"

Artemis paused to give the congregation time to ponder his question.

"Did they cherish it as the wonder that it was? Well, better question would be, do we cherish it for the wonderful gift that it was? Do we look at that helpless babe and feel the love sent from God? Or do we just look at it as a symbol of something that happened long ago, and doesn't have much meaning today?

"Why, some have even done their best to pretend that it never happened." Artemis looked towards the back of the room where Rufus and Richard sat with Gabriel. "They lobby and legislate against the very name of that gift. They want to call this season by any other name than what it is. They want to make this a Winter Holiday and sing songs about snowmen and reindeer, and have special Seasonal Sales, with 50 or 60 percent off of already inflated prices just to get people to become a part of what this time has become. That's what they've done with that gift of love. They can't even say the name of it.

"The name of the Season is CHRISTMAS!" Artemis whispered. " CHRISTMAS!" A little louder. "CHRISTMAS!" Louder still. Someone in the congregation stood and joined him. "CHRISTMAS!" They called out. Soon another, and another stood to join him. All crying out, "CHRISTMAS!" until the room was filled with standing, shouting people. "CHRISTMAS! CHRISTMAS! CHRISTMAS!"

Artemis waited a short while and then signaled for everyone to take their seats. "Yes, the name of the season is Christmas because it signaled the birth of Jesus Christ. And just like those people in His day, some are afraid of that name. Because it means love. And the world today doesn't know how to deal with that kind of gift.

"The world worships other things. Things that are corrupt, things that fade, things that are worthless in God's eyes. When you have the perfect gift, sent from God, to save this world from sin, what more could you want?"

Artemis paused and then spoke quietly. "What do you worship?

"Pray with me. Father, let us never lose sight of the true meaning of this season. Let us never lose sight of the perfect gift that you gave to us. Let the love that you sent fill our hearts and our lives until there is no room for the things of this world. We thank you for the gift of Jesus." Artemis paused for just a second. "Amen," he said, softly.

****

The choir sang their closing number as Artemis made his way to the back of the church where he stood by the door shaking people's hands, giving out a multitude of hugs, and loving the people.

"That was a powerful sermon, Artemis." It was Gabriel.

"Gabriel. Good to see you. It was your inspiration."

"No, Reverend Brown, it was God's inspiration. You just picked it up."

"And I see you have brought a couple of visitors this morning."

That I have, Reverend. This is Rufus Pettifogger and Richard Foster."

"Well now, Mr. Pettifogger I'm familiar with but I think this other fellow used to be known as someone else."

"I was, Reverend Brown." Richard answered. "But it wasn't me. I wasn't really that person."

"That's good, Richard. You know, lots of folks don't really know who they are sometimes. I'm glad you found out."

"Well, I have to give the credit to Gabriel here. He made me see it."

"Ah, yes, Gabriel. It would seem that our friend Gabriel has had a bit of an impact on the town of Newton's Mill."

"Thank you for the compliment." Gabriel laughed.

"Rufus," Artemis turned to him and put out his hand. "I'm very happy to see you here. Would I be wrong to think that you and the OARD have parted company?"

"Yes we have. Thanks to Gabriel."

"Gabriel again. My, my. I think if you plan on staying in Newton's Mill I'm gonna have to build a bigger church."

"Nothin' wrong with that, Reverend." Gabriel laughed as he turned to leave. "I'll see you at the Council meeting on Tuesday."

"I'll be there."

G. D. and Helen had been waiting for Artemis to finish talking to Gabriel. "Artemis, that was quite a sermon. Can't remember when I've seen the folks so wrapped up in what you had to say."

"Thank you, Mr. Mayor. It's always a great service when the people get all caught up in it. Then they get me all fired up. It's a mutual thing."

"I was going to see if you could carve out some time for me today to talk about the Nativity Scene question."

"I'd be happy to."

"Well, after your sermon this morning I think that won't be necessary. It's given me plenty to think about. Thank you."

"You're very welcome, Mr. Mayor. I'll see you at the Council meeting on Tuesday, then."

"Oh yes, I'll be there." G.D. laughed as he and Helen turned to leave. "Along with half the TV and newspaper people in the state."

****

Hebert seldom went to church. Bertha always had one reason or another to keep him busy on Sunday mornings. So it was with a little concern that he made his way to Reverend Brown's church and sat in the very last row. He noticed Gabriel come in with Rufus and another fellow and take a seat near the back of the church.

Looking around he saw that many people he had known for years were there. And he realized that he had really lost touch with so many of the friends he had before he and Bertha were married. Sure, many of them came in the bookstore, but there was a difference in friends who were customers, and friends who were friends. *"I think that's the thing I have missed the most."* He thought, as Artemis got up to speak.

He enjoyed the sermon and was even surprised to find himself on his feet with the rest of the congregation when they began to shout CHRISTMAS!

"Now, why did I do that," He thought, as he sat down. *"Bertha would think I was crazy."* And then another thought entered his mind. *"But wait a minute. I don't have to care what Bertha thinks anymore. I don't have to be concerned that she won't approve of anything I do. I can just go back to being me."*

Hebert started to smile. *"I know what I've missed the most. I've missed me."*

****

"You want to walk home?" Katie asked her Mom. "It's a nice day."

"And then what will we do with the car?"

"Oh, yeah. I forgot we drove."

"Listen, why don't you and Paul walk home and I'll take the car and get dinner started."

"What do you say, Paul? Wanna walk me home?"

"I'm sure you don't have to ask him, Katie." Her Mom laughed.

"Well?"

"Sure, Katie. I'd love to."

"Okay then, kids." Katie's Mom said. "I'll see you at home. Oh, by the way, Katie, stop at the store on the way home and pick up some bread. I think we're out."

"Will do."

Katie's Mom left them and walked to the parking lot. Just as she was getting in the car she noticed Hebert unlocking his car door. "Hebert," she called. "What a surprise to see you in church. Oh my goodness. I didn't mean for that to sound the way it did."

"That's alright, Annie. I was sort of surprised to find myself here, too." Hebert laughed. "It's been a long time."

"Did Bertha come with you?"

"No," Hebert hesitated. "Bertha didn't come with me." Before Bertha had taken over his life Annie and John, the man she eventually married, had been close friends. He decided he felt comfortable telling her what had happened. She would find out soon enough, anyway.

"Annie, Bertha has left me."

"What?"

"Yes. When I got home from the store yesterday there was a packet of papers and a very short note from Bertha. She's filed for divorce and made other legal arrangements to end our relationship, such as it were."

"Oh, Hebert. I'm so sorry."

"Don't be. I have had some time to think about this and I think it's for the best. You know she was never very happy here."

"I know. She never hid her feelings about this town."

"Or about me."

"Do you have any idea what she is going to do?"

"No, but whatever it is it will be in the city. She's always loved it there."

"What about you?"

"Well, she left me the bookstore, and when the house is sold I'll see a little money from that so I'll be alright. I don't need to live in the style to which Bertha had become accustomed."

"Paul, Katie and I are having dinner together this afternoon.

Would you like to come?"

"No, thank you. I really need some time alone to gather my thoughts. There's much to be done. But I'll bet you were surprised to hear about Paul and Katie."

"The only surprise was that it took him so long to get around to it."

"He'll make a fine son-in-law."

"I think so, too. Are you sure you won't join us?"

"Thanks again, Annie, but I think not. Tell Katie I'll see her at the store in the morning. I need to go by and see the Mayor at around nine, so she'll be in charge until I get back."

"Will do, Hebert. Take care."

"You, too, Annie. Goodbye." Hebert got in his car and pulled out of the parking lot.

"So, Bertha left Hebert." She thought as she watched him go. *"Well, the loss is hers."*

****

"Hello Katie, Paul." Galena Bauxite was at the checkout stand when the two young people placed the loaf of bread on the conveyor belt. "Did you find everything okay?"

"Sure did, Galena." Katie answered. "How are you today?"

"Well, except for my feet hurting from standing on them all day, and my back giving me trouble for the same reason, and a little cold in my head I suppose I'm as well as can be expected." Then Galena began laughing. "I'm just joking, Katie. I'm really feeling great. You two both look like the cat that ate the canary. What's going on?"

"Paul asked me to marry him." Katie giggled.

"Well, it's about time."

"Come on, Galena, give me break, okay." Paul begged. "I can't help it if I take my time doing things."

"Well, all I've got to say is you're lucky that while you were taking your time somebody else didn't scoop this girl up and carry her off."

"There wouldn't have been much chance of that." Katie said. "I was planning on waiting for as long as it took."

"I guess you got lucky, Paul."

"I sure did."

"So, when is the big day?"

"We haven't set a date yet. This only happened yesterday."

"Yesterday, eh? I suppose you'll want a June wedding. Seems like girls just like June weddings."

"We hadn't talked about it but I think June would be nice. What do you think, Paul."

"Well, uh, yeah, I guess June would be okay."

"From the look on his face I'd say he was thinking of a much closer date. Right, Paul?"

Paul stood quietly, without answering. The people behind them in line and at the next check stand had all stopped talking and were listening closely to this conversation. And enjoying it greatly.

"Paul?" Katie asked. "Did you want to get married sooner than that?"

"Katie, can we talk about this somewhere else besides here in front of all these people?"

For the first time Katie realized that everyone was listening in and now her face grew a lovely shade of crimson. "Uh, how much do we owe you for the bread, Galena?"

"That'll be two dollars and fourteen cents, Katie." Galena placed the bread in a plastic bag and handed it to Paul.

"Here you go." Katie gave the money to Galena, grabbed Paul by the arm and hurried toward the door.

"Congratulations, Katie." Galena called after them. "And you, too, Paul."

When they were outside and away from the store Katie asked Paul. "Was Galena right? Do you want to get married sooner than June?"

"Katie, I know I'm shy, and even a little slow." Paul answered quietly.

"You're shy, alright. But you're not slow. You're just..."

"Slow." Paul interrupted her. "But when it comes to you it's even worse. I care so much for you that sometimes it scares me. I get all tongue tied when I'm around you. I can't think straight. And I would marry you tomorrow, if it were up to me."

Paul's outburst surprised Katie. She knew he cared for her but she hadn't understood just how deep those feelings were. She slipped her arm in his and they walked along in silence for awhile.

"I would marry you tomorrow, too." She said softly, holding his arm even tighter.

****

Things were going from bad to worse for Ira Freethinker. His picketing plan was a disaster, the newspaper wouldn't have anything to do with the ad he wanted to run, he lost the only other member of his organization, his confrontation with the Mayor went badly and now, as he was sitting in the coffee shop nursing a hot chocolate, Gabriel walked in.

"Oh no," He thought, swiveling around in his chair so he wouldn't be recognized.

"Hello, Ira."

Too late. Gabriel had not only seen him, but he was sitting down in the other chair at his table.

"How's the hot chocolate?"

"I don't really want to talk to you." Ira said, without looking at him.

"That's okay. I want to talk to you."

"I won't listen."

"That's okay, too. I'll talk anyway."

Ira started to get up to leave but Gabriel put his hand on his arm and suddenly his legs grew weak and he collapsed in the chair. He couldn't move. It was as if something held him there.

"Ira, you know, you're not the first person to deny the existence of God. And you probably won't be the last. History is full of people who proclaimed that God did not exist. In fact some even went so far as to say that God was dead. And, today, there are many people who live as if there were no God. They waste their lives on things that don't last."

In spite of himself Ira hung on every word. Gabriel's voice

seemed different somehow. Not harsh, or accusing. But calm and even. Almost soothing. Ira fought to maintain his resistance to what Gabriel was saying.

"Yesterday the Mayor asked you what you believed in. And you couldn't answer him."

"Wait a minute. How do you know that? You weren't there." Ira asked.

"That's not important. What is important is the answer to the question. What do you believe in Ira Freethinker? What have you ever believed in?"

Once again Ira was stumped for an answer. He couldn't remember whether he had ever believed in anything. So he just sat silently.

"Because you have never asked yourself that question you have no answer for it. And now it may be too late for you to find the answer. God has the answer. But you must believe in Him. If you don't, then there is no answer for you. At least not now. But, there will be Ira. Yes, someday there will be. And I fear it won't be the answer you want, or expect."

"What do you mean?" Ira asked.

"What if you're wrong, Ira? What will you do if the time comes and you discover that you have been wrong all these years, and there really is a God?"

Once again Ira had no answer.

"Well, Ira, when that time comes you will have plenty of time to think about your mistake."

"Plenty of time?"

"Yes," Gabriel stood up to leave. "An eternity."

****

J. B. Nickels stood at his office window looking out at the parking lot. Sunday mornings were always slow at the Mall. Nearly everyone in town went to church. J.B. and Cora used to go too, until he decided that there was money to be made on Sunday, same as any other day. Before that most of the stores in the Mall closed their doors on that day but when J.B. decided to be open a lot of the other stores followed suit. Only Hebert's bookstore stayed closed on Sunday.

"I'm surprised Bertha let him get away with that." He thought. *"I guess she just didn't take much of an interest in anything Hebert did."* In a way, J.B. felt sorry for Hebert. Or, at least he felt something similar to sorry. It was an unfamiliar feeling to him. But since yesterday there were a lot of new feelings that he wasn't used to. He had changed. Something many folks would have bet a month's salary would never happen. He and Cora had spent most

of the evening talking, something the seldom did before. But, it seemed, now all J. B. wanted to do was sit and talk with her. It surprised him just how much about Cora he didn't know, or had forgotten. While they talked he saw in his mind the pretty, dark haired girl that took his breath away the first time he saw her in Biology class his Freshman year. And he realized just how much he loved this woman who had put up with him all these years.

"Cora," He had said to her. "Do you have any idea how much I love you?"

Cora sat silently for a long while, just looking at him. He noticed the beginning of a tear forming in the corner of her eye. *"Great, I've made her cry."* He thought.

"James Brewster Nickels," Cora spoke softly, using his full name. Something she only did when she was angry. " I've known how you felt about me ever since that afternoon when you stole a kiss in the movie theater."

J.B. smiled at the thought.

"But, I must admit, there have been times over these past twenty years or so when I had my doubts. When I thought you cared more for the store, and the money, than you did for me. And I almost gave up hope that the man I fell in love with would find his way back to me. But you did."

"Thanks to that fellow Gabriel." J.B. answered.

"Yes, thanks to that fellow Gabriel. And he was pleased to hear about the change in you when I told him."

"You talked to him?"

"Yes, I was having my lunch in the courtyard of the Mall and he came and sat down next to me. You know, that's strange, now that I think of it."

"What's that?"

"Well, he said he had heard I was looking for him."

"That's not unusual."

"Maybe not. But Finster had just left to find him for me when he showed up. Couldn't have been more than a half minute."

"Well, Maybe Finster ran into him right away."

"I might think that except Finster went in one direction and Gabriel came from the other."

"That does seem strange."

"Well, anyway, I told him about our conversation of the morning and how much you had changed since talking with him."

"And?"

"I told him I had been trying to get through to you for years with basically the same thing he told you, without much success."

"I know. I just wasn't ready to hear that, yet. So what did he say?"

"He said sometimes it wasn't the message, but the messenger that made the difference."

"That seems a strange thing for him to say."

"Not so strange. Do you remember what Gabriel means?"

"I suppose I should, but no, I can't recall."

"It means God's messenger."

"That's right. Say, maybe that's why he seems to show up so unexpectedly some times."

"Because?"

"Because he's an angel. Oh, I know that sounds far fetched. But it would explain how he is always in the right place at the right time."

Cora thought about that for a minute. She remembered Finster's conversation with her about Gabriel, and what he had suggested to him about the Santa problem. And J.B.'s encounter with Gabriel and her own meeting with him. Maybe there was something to this angel thing.

"You know, J.B., that might not be too far fetched after all."

The phone interrupted his thoughts. He turned from the

window, sat down at the desk and picked up the phone.

"Hello, J.B. here."

"Mr. Nickels, it's Finster."

"Yes?"

"I've got some good news. I was able to convince three of the Santas that quit to come back to work. Now we have enough to get us through the rest of the season."

"That's great news, Alan."

He had never called him by his first name before.

"J.B., are you okay?"

"Oh yes, Alan. I'm okay. In fact, I'm very okay." J.B. began to chuckle as he hung up the phone. "Yes, I am very, very okay."

****

It had been a long day for Hebert. After church he went home, fixed himself some lunch and then sat for at the table for awhile. He was still having trouble coming to grips with all of these sudden changes. He had known that Bertha was unhappy with her life in Newton's Mill, and that he was a disappointment to her. *"I never expected her to take such a drastic move."* He thought. *"But she had been getting worse lately. I almost hated to come home after work."*

Hebert looked over the packet of papers that Bertha had left, making sure that he understood everything that was there. His meeting with the Mayor in the morning would help him form a plan of action.

After a short while he got up from the table, rinsed his dishes and put them in the dishwasher. Then he went upstairs to Bertha's room. Standing in the middle of the room he realized just how little he had been in it over the many years of their marriage. It felt strange to him.

Empty.

It was a big bedroom. The biggest room in the house except for the living room. The huge four-poster bed that had belonged to her parents sat against one wall, and a dresser sat in one corner of the room. The door to the massive closet that had held Bertha's things stood open and it was a bit of a surprise just how large it was. "Why, it's nearly as big as my bedroom." He said, with a chuckle. "I guess I know who rated around here. Well, Bertha, someone will love this old house. Much more than you, or I, have. I won't be sad to see it sold. It'll give me a new start, too. And the sooner the better."

The rest of the evening was spent in going through the house deciding what would be sold and what he would keep for himself. When he finally came to the last few items in the basement he realized just how few things he would be taking with him. *"Not much to show for all these years of marriage."* He thought. *"And not much in the way of memories, either. At least not many good ones."* And for the first time Hebert realized something that he had ignored. He realized just how unhappy he had been.

****

"I'm heading up to bed, G.D." Helen said. "Are you coming?"

"I'll be up in a minute. Got a couple of things I want to do before I hit the sack."

"Okay, but don't be too long. It's late."

G. D. got up and went to the front door. Opening it quietly he stepped outside and shut it softly behind him. He walked over to the porch railing and stood looking out at the town of Newton's Mill. There was never much going on in this end of town at this time of night. This was old town. Most of the houses here had been built at the time of the Mill, and although they were old, the people who lived in them felt a particular pride in keeping them looking nice.

"These old houses have character." Sam Barnes had told him one day. "Not like those cookie cutter houses over in the newer part of town. I don't see how they can tell one from the other."

G.D. had to agree with him. There was a world of difference in the two areas. The newer part of town had wide streets, and large houses, with big yards, and fences. There were no fences in the old part of town. And because there were no fences neighbors knew each other. So it wasn't unusual when G.D. noticed Nate Archibald out walking his dog.

"Evenin', Nate." He called out.

"Oh, hey, G.D. what are you doing out on the porch at this hour of the night?"

"Just getting a little fresh air before going up to bed. I see your out for an evening walk."

"No, G. D., Max here is out for his evening walk. I'm just along for company, I guess."

"Well, it's a nice night for it."

"Sure is. Little chilly, though. Say, G. D. have you thought any more about your decision?"

"Constantly."

"And?"

"And you'll find out Tuesday night."

"Okay, G.D." Nate laughed. "I guess I can wait. Just a couple more days."

"Thanks, I didn't need to be reminded."

Max began to pull the Councilman away. "I'll be seeing you G. D. Looks like Max wants to walk me some more."

"Good night, Archie, Max. Enjoy." But the dog had pulled Archie beyond hearing.

Archie was right. It was a little chilly. One of those cold crisp nights, with no moon and the sky full of stars. *"Must have been a night like this when the angels visited the shepherds."* He thought. *"Man, I'll bet that was scary. Shepherds half asleep, sheep all quiet and then bang, a sky full of angels. It's a wonder they didn't all have heart attacks."*

"Evenin' Mr. Mayor."

"Huh?" G.D. started. "Who is it?"

"Just me." Gabriel stepped out of the darkness. "Beautiful night, isn't it?"

"Gabriel, you sure do get around. What are you doing out here?"

"Taking my evening walk and looking at the stars. I always like to spend some time looking at the heavens. It's comforting."

"Comforting?"

"Yes. There's a feeling of eternity there. A permanence. Just realizing how long they have been there. And how each one was placed just where it's supposed to be."

"Oh, yes. I remember. In the book of Genesis. At the time of creation."

"And God said, 'Let bright lights appear in the sky to separate the day from the night. They will be signs to mark off the seasons, the days and the years.' and so he put each star in it's place."

"I was just thinking to myself how frightened the shepherds must have been when the angels first appeared to them."

"They fell on their faces, at first. But when I...I mean when the angel told them not to be afraid their fears were calmed and they were amazed at what they were told."

"You know, Gabriel, you sound almost like you were there."
Gabriel didn't answer.

"I've often wondered," G.D. continued. "Why did the angels go to the shepherds? Why didn't they announce the birth of Jesus to the leaders of Israel?"

"Because He didn't come for the kings and rulers of this world. He came for the shepherds, and the slaves, and the people who were without hope. That little baby, in an animal feeding trough, in an animal shelter carved in the side of a hill, was the hope of the nations. Who better to be the first hearers of the good news than the very people He came to save."

"I suppose so."

"You know, Mr. Mayor." Gabriel continued. "That's why the Nativity Scene has become so controversial. So many people today are frightened by the symbol."

"Frightened?"

"Yes. But it's not unusual. Ever since His birth Jesus and His message have frightened people. Because He speaks of love, and forgiveness. Concepts which are hard for them to accept. The rulers of that day feared Him because of His compassion for the people. And His opposition to them. He blamed them for perverting the Law to suit their own ends. They saw their hold on the people threatened."

"So they conspired to kill Him."

"Right. And today there are people who are conspiring to kill Him again."

"How do you mean?"

"By opposing His message any where and any way they can. You've seen the trend. Banning prayer in schools, removing the Ten Commandments from public display, filing lawsuits against any thing that has a Christian theme or basis."

"And Nativity Scenes."

"And that, too. It seems to grow more and more every day."

"I would think that God would be tired of it."

"He is." Gabriel said, as he walked away.

****

Monday

"Good morning, Mr. H." Katie said, as she entered the bookstore.

"Good morning, Katie. How are you this morning?"

"Well, I'm fine but I think a more important question is how are you? My Mom shared your conversation with her after Church on Sunday. I was really shocked."

"That makes two of us. But, I guess I should have seen this coming. I knew Bertha wasn't happy, and her running off to the city when things didn't go right should have given me a clue. I guess I just didn't want to see it."

"So, once again, how are you?"

Hebert thought for a moment before answering. "I suppose I'm a lot better than I should be."

"What do you mean?"

"A man who has just had his wife walk out on him, take all her belongings with her and draw up papers to sell the house should be feeling a lot worse than I am."

"A lot worse?"

"Yes. Strangely enough I think in the back of my mind I had expected this. And now that it has happened I am surprised at my feelings."

"In what way?"

"I'm relieved. The tension of all those years of never being able to get anything right, never making Bertha happy, never having children and never being my own man is all stripped away now. Bertha did me a huge favor. But I'm sure she wouldn't agree."

"I will say, you don't look like you're suffering."

"I guess I don't, do I." Hebert laughed. "You know, this is the first morning in as long as I can remember that I didn't wake up with a headache."

"Because your headache wasn't home." Katie said, with a twinkle in her eye. She was happy that Hebert was taking this turn of events so well. She really cared for him and was worried that it might be more than he could handle.

"That's good, Katie." Hebert gave her a hug. "Now, I'm glad you're here. You'll have to mind the store for a bit. I've asked the

Mayor to look over all these documents that Bertha left me to make sure everything is in order. I'm due at his office at 9:00 so I think I'll leave now and grab a cup of coffee before I see him."

"Righto, Mr. H. I've got everything under control. See you when you get back."

Katie watched Hebert leave the store and turn in the direction of the coffee shop. *"I was worried that all this would be too much for Mr. H."* She thought. *"But it looks like he's stronger than I thought."*

****

G. D. had slept really well. The fresh air and his talk with Gabriel had been good. He was smiling as he came downstairs to breakfast.

"Well now," Helen said from where she was cooking breakfast. "Don't you look like the cat that ate the canary. Why the big smile."

"Oh, no reason. I just feel great this morning."

"You seem to have slept okay. In fact, I had a little trouble waking you."

"I slept great, I feel great, you look great and it's gonna be a great day."

"Great." Helen laughed. "Now, wrap yourself around these

pancakes and get to work. I've got work to do around here to get ready for Christmas."

G. D. finished his pancakes, poured another cup of coffee in a Styrofoam cup, picked up the newspaper and headed for the door.

"I'm out of here, Helen. See you later." He called as he left.

"Wait a minute, G.D." Helen called out from the laundry room. "I have a grocery list for you. There are some things I'll need on your way home tonight."

Helen handed him a sheet of paper, gave him a peck on the cheek and shoved him out the door.

"I'll miss you, too." G.D. said with a smile.

****

"Hello, Chief?" Ira Freethinker was on the phone to the headquarters of the Atheists and Agnostics Association. "Ira Freethinker here."

"What do want, Freethinker? I'm a busy man." The chief wasn't too fond of Ira. He thought him ineffective as a representative for AAA.

"Just wanted to touch base with you and fill you in on how things are going here."

"So, how are they going?"

"Not good."

"What? What do you mean not good?"

"I mean this is turning out to be a very difficult assignment."

"Freethinker, Newton's Mill is a little dinky, one horse town. All you have to do is make sure that they don't put that Nativity Scene on the courthouse lawn."

"I know, chief. I know. It's just that things keep getting in my way. Every where I turn there's another roadblock.."

"Explain."

"Well, the city council vote was a two for, two against tie and the Mayor has the tie breaker."

"So?"

"So, tomorrow night is the next meeting and I'm not sure just how he is going to vote."

"Did you picket City Hall?"

"Yes, on Saturday."

"Saturday? Nobody works at City Hall on Saturday!"

"I know that. But by the time I got the picket signs made it was late Friday night."

"Didn't you tell the sign maker when you needed them?"

"Yes."

"So why were they late?"

"None of the sign makers in town would do them. I wound up making them myself."

"You made them yourself?"

"Yes sir. So the earliest we could get to City Hall was Saturday."

"Alright. Did you get the ad in the newspaper?"

"No sir."

"What?"

"I said, no sir. I didn't get the ad in the newspaper."

"Why not?"

"The editor wouldn't run it."

"The editor wouldn't run it?"

"No sir. I should add that she was one of the ones that voted for the Nativity Scene."

"That's a violation of our freedom of speech. Did you tell her that?"

"Yes sir."

"And what did she say about that?"

"She wasn't very nice."

"Freethinker, I want you and that assistant of yours, what's his name? Oh, yes, Phil Faithless. I want you and Faithless out in front of that City Council meeting tomorrow night with your picket signs. There will be TV and newspaper people from all over the country. This is a big thing, Freethinker. This could make us or break us as far as our battle against Christians and every thing they stand for is concerned. So I want the two of you..."

"One of me." Ira interrupted.

"What did you say?"

"I said there is just one of me."

"What happened to that Faithless fellow?"

"Well, I think he lost the courage of his convictions."

"Just what do you mean by that?"

"Chief, there's this fellow here in town. Big guy. Very imposing. Anyway. He had a talk with Phil and the next thing I know Phil and him are gone. And I'm left holding two picket signs."

"So, your all by yourself there?"

"Yes sir, and it's kind of lonely."

"Get a hold of yourself, Freethinker. You have an important job. You can't let a little setback get you down." The Chief didn't like the way this was sounding. He knew Freethinker was a bit of a washout, but he was all he had to send. The Atheists and Agnostics Society was a very small operation. Very small.

"I could use some help, Chief."

"Freethinker, I have no one to send there. You know we're a small group. And our representatives are stretched very thin."

"But, just one more person would give us a little more clout. It looks so weak with just me picketing. I get laughed at a lot."

"There just isn't anyone to send. I'll be very candid with you, Freethinker. Counting you and me there are only six of us in the organization."

"Only six? I thought we we're a national presence? A force to be reckoned with. At least that's what you told me when I signed up."

"Ah, yes, well, we are a national organization. I'm here, you're there and we have a representative in California, one in Washington, and two in jail in Chicago."

"In jail?"

"Yes, our last protest got a little out of hand. But that's neither here nor there. You have a job to do, Freethinker. Get on it." The phone went dead.

"Only six people, and two of them are in jail?" Ira said, as he hung up the phone. "I think I've made a big mistake. Maybe Gabriel was right. I've spent so much time proclaiming what I don't believe in that I've never stopped to think about what I do believe in."

Ira put on his coat and left his hotel room. He made his way to the Mall and got himself a sandwich at the Underground Shoppe. He found a seat at a table at the back and began to eat.

"Hello, Ira."

"Hello, Gabriel." Ira said, without looking up. "I figured you'd show up."

"Rough day?"

"Very."

"Want to talk about it?"

"That would be good."

Ira spent the next few minutes telling Gabriel about his phone call and the surprising news about the size of the AAA. Gabriel sat and listened quietly. When he was done Gabriel reached over and put his hand on Ira's arm. He didn't feel the same sensation that he had the last time Gabriel had touched his arm. This time it was a comforting feeling.

"Ira, I'm sorry about the bad news. But maybe now you can spend some time deciding what you do believe in. And believing in God would be good for starters."

"That's just it, Gabriel. I don't know what I believe in. I've spent so much time telling everyone that God doesn't exist I'm not sure I really can believe in Him."

"Well, Ira. He believes in you."

"What?"

"I said God believes in you. He believes in the goodness of your heart. Something that I think you aren't even aware of."

"The goodness of my heart? Gabriel, I don't think there is any goodness in my heart."

"There is. God put it there. You just have to find it. We'll talk again." And Gabriel walked away, leaving Ira sitting alone.

****

"I really appreciate you taking the time to look over these things for me, G.D." Hebert said as he sat down in front of the Mayor's desk. "A lot of it is pretty involved and I'm not real sharp when it comes to legal stuff."

"Happy to help, Hebert." G.D. said as he picked up the brown envelope Hebert had put on the desk. "Let's take a look at these."

G.D. spent a few minutes going over the pile of documents that had been in the envelope.

"These are very thorough. Hebert. Bertha seems to have thought of everything."

"She always did."

"You have to put the house up for sale as soon as possible. I don't imagine you'll have much trouble selling it."

"I'm going to contact Carl Oglethorpe over at Newton's Mill Realty as soon as I leave here. I've already started setting aside things to get rid of. It seems Bertha wanted nothing of our life together except her clothes."

"That's the way it looks from these documents. How are you going to dispose of the stuff? A yard sale?"

"Oh, not a chance. I hate those things. I'm going to give everything to charity. I know the homeless shelter can use a lot of it. It's mostly in excellent condition."

"Have you thought about where you're going to live?"

"Not yet. But I can stay in the house until it's sold. That will give me time to make arrangements. I should be able to find something by then."

"You might check with Carl. I'm sure he knows of some places that are available."

"Good idea."

"Hebert, I must say you're taking this all pretty well."

"I don't have much choice, G.D. Bertha started this ball rolling, I'm just staying one step ahead of it so it doesn't run me over. But I must admit, I'm not as upset as you would think. In fact, I'm ..." Hebert paused as if searching for a word. "I guess the word I'm looking for is free."

"Free?"

" Yes. For the first time in a long, long time I am my own person. I don't have to be what Bertha thinks I should be. I was just thinking last night. I've missed me."

"Well, Hebert, we've missed you, too. And if there is anything we can do to make this situation any easier, just let us know."

"You can do one thing for me, G.D."

"What's that?"

"Vote in favor of the Nativity Scene tomorrow night. I know I can't change my vote but if things had been different I would have voted for it. It's an important part of Newton's Mill."

"You know, Hebert." G.D. smiled. "I wish things had been

different, too. Then I wouldn't have to be the tie breaking vote."

"Well, I know you will vote for whatever is best for Newton's Mill. And I'll be there to support you, whichever way you vote."

"Thank you." G.D. got up and came around the desk. He shook Hebert's hand and the two of them walked to the door of his office. "I'll see you tomorrow night." He said as Hebert left.

"Goodbye Councilman Humble." Jayne said as Hebert walked out.

"Goodbye Jane. And it's Hebert, please."

"Right. Hebert. Have a good day." Jayne called after him.

"Jayne." G.D. spoke from the door of his office.'

" Yes, Mr. Mayor."

"Get Mary Beth Johnson on the phone for me. please."

"Right away." Jayne dialed the number of the Newton's Mill Press as G. D. went back into his office and shut the door. Just as he sat down at the desk the intercom buzzed.

"Yes, Jayne?"

"Mary Beth's on line one."

"Thank you." G.D. picked up the receiver and punched the blinking light.

"Mary Beth?"

"Good morning, G.D. What's up?"

"Hebert Humble just left my office. Did you hear about him and Bertha?"

"I'm afraid I did. You know it doesn't take long for news to travel in this town. I sometimes wonder why I bother with the newspaper. Everybody knows what's going on before the paper does."

"That's Newton's Mill alright. But here's what I wanted to run by you."

"Shoot."

"Can we keep all of that out of the papers? Hebert is handling it all pretty well but I'm not sure how he would take it if the situation was spread out there for everyone to see."

"I had already decided that I wouldn't print anything about it. I've known Hebert a long time and I would never do anything to hurt him."

"I was hoping you would say that. Now, I want to talk to you about tomorrow night."

"The Council meeting?"

"Yes. You know that there are going to be TV reporters and newspaper people from all over the state here?"

"Oh yes, I've had at least a dozen calls on that very subject the last couple of days. Looks like our little problem is turning into a big problem."

"Can you believe it? Isn't there any other news out there that's more important than what the little town of Newton's Mill does with its Nativity Scene?"

"G.D. I don't think you've grasped the significance of this whole issue."

"Really?"

"There's more to it than just our little Nativity Scene. It's the whole issue of Christmas. There are certain groups that want to put an end to the message that the Nativity Scene brings. The message of hope no matter how crazy and dysfunctional this old world gets. And they've been at it for 2000 years."

"But it seems to be getting worse."

"I know. Every day, here at the paper, I get bulletins from many different places around the world. The assault on Christians and what we believe in goes on daily. At least, so far, they're not killing us here, yet."

"Yet. But in some ways they are killing us. Bit by bit. Did you know that Ira Freethinker was picketing City Hall?"

"He was in here on Friday wanting to run an ad in the paper about the Nativity Scene and the fact that it was an ethnic folk tale and there wasn't really any God and all that sort of trash."

"Really? What did you do?"

"I threw him out."

"Well, he was picketing City Hall on Saturday morning."

"Saturday? Doesn't he know nobody works down there on Saturday?"

"That's what I asked him. Funny thing, though."

"What's that?"

"Well, I guess his partner, Phil Faithless, had been there with him but he was gone when I got there."

"Gone? Get to cold for him?"

"No, Ira said he lost his sense of direction."

"That is interesting. Did he say how that came about?"

"Yes. Said he had been talking to this new fellow in town. Gabriel. And he convinced Phil that what he was doing was wrong."

"I've been hearing stories about this Gabriel. Have you talked to him?"

"Yes, several times. He is a very interesting fellow. Maybe you will run in to him one of these days. In fact, if he knows you're looking for him it wouldn't surprise me if he just showed up."

"What?"

"Trust me. I know what I'm talking about."

"Well, I would like to talk to him so if you see him have him stop by the paper."

"I'll do that. See you tomorrow night, Mary Beth." G.D. hung up.

"I've a hunch that Mary Beth is going to see this Gabriel sooner than she thinks." He thought.

****

Just as Mary Beth hung up the phone her intercom buzzed. "Yes, Carol, what is it?"

"Someone here to see you. Says his name is Gabriel."

"Well," Mary Beth said softly. "That was fast."

"What did you say?"

"Nothing, Carol. Why don't you send him in?"

"Right away."

The fellow that came through the door was big alright. Mary Beth got up from behind her desk to meet him. *"I barely come up to his chest."* She thought.

"Hello, Gabriel. I've been hoping we could meet. I've heard a lot about you."

"I hope it hasn't been anything bad. I wouldn't want it to get in your paper."

"It's all been good. What can I do for you?"

"I wanted to stop in and thank you for not running that ad from the AAA."

"How did you know about that?"

"Oh, I have my sources. That took some courage to refuse the ad."

"I know, freedom of speech and all that. But, this is still my newspaper and I make those decisions. There was no way I was going to let that group advertise their hatred in it. That Ira Freethinker is a real piece of work."

"Yes, well, Ira may be having second thoughts about his involvement with that group."

"How's that?"

Gabriel told Mary Beth about his conversation with Phil on Saturday and then with Ira just a few minutes ago. "I think Ira is facing a big decision. At least for him."

"Gabriel, you're new in town, aren't you?"

"Yes, I've actually been here just since last Tuesday. I was at the City Council meeting."

"Funny, I didn't see you there. And a fellow as big as you would be hard to miss."

"I was in the back of the chambers, near the door to the hallway. It was a very interesting meeting."

"Yes, it was. Very interesting. I just wish we had been able to deal with the Nativity Scene then without putting all this pressure on the Mayor."

"I don't think I would worry too much about G.D. Steward. He seems to be a very fair and levelheaded person."

"Oh, he is that. That's what makes this so tough. He's well aware that he represents all the people of Newton's Mill and whatever decision he makes he knows some folks aren't going to agree with it."

"True, but making tough decisions is part of being a leader, or a newspaper publisher, or the owner of the biggest store this side of the city to the East. It just goes with the territory."

"Still, sometimes it's hard to know what is right."

"Most of the time. But, sometimes, what's right is so obvious that the decision is almost made for you. And I think that the Mayor knows what the right decision is. And I think he will be strong enough to make it."

"Well, I hope you're right."

"I suppose we will just have to wait until tomorrow night to find out."

"Will you be there?"

"Absolutely. I wouldn't miss it for the world. Well, I should be on my way. I know you're busy and I still have a few things to do today myself."

"It's been nice talking to you, Gabriel. See you tomorrow night."

"That you will. That you will. It should be a very interesting meeting."

****

"Humble's Book Emporium. Katie speaking. How can I help you?"

"Katie, It's Hebert."

"Oh, Hi Mr. H. What's up?"

"I'm on my way to see Carl Oglethorpe over at Newton's Mill Realty to start the paperwork for selling my house. How are things there at the store?"

"Kind of quiet right now. It's early yet."

"Can you handle it for awhile without me?"

"Sure can, Mr. H. You just do what you have to do and don't worry about things down here."

"You're a good girl, Katie. I sure made a smart move when I hired you."

"Oh, I'll bet you tell that to all your clerks." Katie laughed. "Oops, here's a customer. I'll see you when you get back."

"Okay, Katie. Goodbye."

Katie hung up the phone and turned to the man who had just entered the store.

"Wow," she thought. *"This is one big guy."*

"Good morning, Katie."

"Uh, good morning. But, how do you know my name?"

"Hebert has told me all about you and how lucky he is to have you for his assistant. My name is Gabriel and I just wanted to stop in and talk with you for a minute."

"Nice to meet you, Gabriel. What did you want to talk about?"

"You know that Hebert is going through a tough time right now?"

"You mean about Bertha?"

"Yes. His whole life is changing."

"For the better, I think."

"Yes, I'm sure you're right. Bertha was a source of much unhappiness for him."

"Funny thing, though. No matter how tough things got at home he was always calm and friendly here at the store."

"That's because, deep down inside, he has a very good heart."

"That's for sure."

"What I wanted to ask you is if you would do your best to help him get through this?"

"He seems to be holding up pretty good right now."

"He is. But he is going to need friends to support him and keep him positive about this whole thing."

"Well, he sure has lots of friends. My Mom thinks the world of him."

"It would seem that many others feel that way. Maybe when this is all over he will have a chance to enjoy some of those friendships."

"I hope so. Bertha pretty much kept him under her thumb. He seemed to really enjoy coming here to the store. And he's great with the customers."

"Then, I can count on you to do what you can to help him through this?"

"I would have even if you hadn't asked me."

"Good. I was sure you would be happy to help. By the way, I hear you're getting married."

"Yep, just as soon as I can pin Paul down on a date. I'm thinking June."

"Well, that's not too far away. Paul is a very nice young man. The two of you will be very happy."

"I hope so."

"Oh, don't worry. I'm sure of it." Gabriel said as he turned to leave. "Yes, I'm very sure of it."

"I wonder what he meant by that?" Katie thought as she watched him go.

****

"Well, tomorrow's the big day." Helen said to G. D. as she

crawled into bed beside him. "Have you decided which way you will vote at the meeting?"

"Not exactly"

"Want to talk about it?"

"No, I don't think so."

"Why not?"

"Because I'm still forming the response in my mind and I don't want anything to sidetrack me. I've had a whole week to agonize over this and so many people have tried to have an input into it that it's about to drive me crazy."

"A good night's sleep should help, don't you think?"

"I hope so. Goodnight, Helen."

"Goodnight, sweetie."

"If those Christmas ghost guys show up tonight," G.D. thought as he drifted off to sleep. *"I'll go stark raving mad."*

****

"Mr. Mayor." The voice came to G.D. in his sleep.

"Oh no, not again." He sat up in bed and looked around. But there was no one in the room. Helen was sound asleep, and the house was quiet. "Hmm, must have been hearing things." He started to lie back down when he heard the voice again.

"Mr. Mayor." It almost sounded like Gabriel's voice.

"Gabriel, is that you?" He whispered. "And what are you doing in my bedroom?"

"Where is Christmas, Mr. Mayor?"

"What?"

"Where is Christmas?"

"What kind of a question is that?"

"A very important one. Where is Christmas?"

"Well, lately it's pretty plain to see. It's in crowds of shoppers, and spending, and buying. And Santa Claus in Nickel's department store, and a tree full of presents." G.D. was just getting started. "And parties, and debt, lots of debt that makes you crazy when the bills start coming in. It's Christmas cards from people you don't talk to all year, and kids leaving cookies and milk for some fat guy in a red suit that doesn't even exist."

G.D. suddenly realized that he was angry.

"Gabriel, I used to love Christmas. But it's just not Christmas anymore, and I have to make a decision that could mean the end of Christmas. I don't want Newton's Mill to be the town that forgot Christmas."

G.D. heard the voice once again.

"Mr. Mayor, all those things aren't Christmas. So I ask you again where is Christmas?"

G.D. sat quietly for a moment. Then he began to speak softly.

"You're right Gabriel. Christmas isn't all those things. Those are what we've made it. No, Christmas is a stable, with the wonderful gift of a Savior lying in a rough feeding trough. It's about angels, and shepherds, and hope. And it's about love. Oh yes, it's about love. That's really what Christmas is all about."

"So then," the voice asked again. "Do you know where Christmas is?"

"Yes, yes. I do know. Christmas is in the hearts of men."

G.D. waited for the voice but all was quiet. He slowly lay back down and pulled the covers up to his chin. "Christmas is in the hearts of men." He said, as he fell into a deep sleep.

****

Tuesday

"Good evening Ladies and Gentlemen. This is Randal "Scoop" Peterson of The Evening News here at the Newton's Mill City Council Meeting. Right now we're outside of the Court House awaiting the arrival of the council members and, of course, the Mayor. It will be up to Mayor Steward to break the deadlock over the placement of the Nativity Scene in front of this very courthouse. The controversy in this small town has had major implications around the country as other communities watch to see if the concept of the traditional Christmas will survive. The council chambers are packed with local citizens, as well as TV and newspaper reporters from around the state. We have set up shop here on the steps of the courthouse while our associate, Verna Dickerson, is covering the proceedings from inside the council chambers. Verna, how are things in there?"

"Well, Scoop, pretty crowded. Every seat is full and there are people standing up along the walls and filling the hallway."

"Have you had a chance to talk to anyone yet?"

"Yes, several folks have been more than happy to give me their opinions on this situation."

"What's the consensus?"

"There isn't one. The whole crowd seems to be equally divided over the subject. But it does seem that the long time residents of Newton's Mill are overwhelmingly in favor of the Nativity Scene taking it's traditional place in front of the courthouse. While many of the newcomers to town seem to be ambivalent about it. They just want to see what happens. Back to you Scoop."

"Thanks Verna. Very interesting. It seems the Mayor has been unavailable for comment this entire week as he struggles with his decision. Sources close to the Mayor, however, have stated that as late as last night it was not clear just how he would vote. Oh, just a minute. I see councilman Nathaniel Archibald coming up the walk."

Archie saw the reporter from halfway down the block.

"Councilman Archibald" Peterson stopped Archie just before he started up the steps.

"Why, Hello Scoop." Nate smiled his biggest politician's smile.

"You know me?" Scoop questioned.

"Of course. As a City Councilman charged with the responsibility of running this fair city it is only natural that I would know important people like yourself."

"Well, thank you, Councilman." Scoop was flattered to think that he was well known in Newton's Mill. "Can you give me a statement about tonight's meeting?"

" Oh, it's an important meeting. Yes indeed, very important. I, of course, voted in favor of the Nativity Scene being placed in front of the Court House. It is a long tradition here in our town, dating back to when the Mill was the major employer and the late Colonel Newton proudly displayed it in front of his establishment. And so, as a representative of the people of this fair town I..."

"Thank you, Councilman." Scoop interrupted Archie. "I think they're waiting for you inside."

"Ah, yes. Yes indeed I'm sure they are. Thank you so much, Scoop. It's been a pleasure talking to you." Archie waved at the camera and made his way inside.

"That was Councilman Nathaniel Archibald. Well known for his oratory. By the way, Verna?"

"Yes Scoop."

"Archibald is on his way inside. Keep him away from the microphone."

"Will do, Scoop. Oh oh, he's heading my way."

"We'll just keep you off air until he runs down."

"Maybe by the time the meeting starts. I hope."

"Here comes the Mayor, now. I'm going to try and get a

statement from him." Scoop positioned himself in front of G. D. and, shoved the microphone up to his face. "Mr. Mayor, I'm Scoop Peterson of the Channel 84 Evening News..."

"I know who you are, Scoop, and you're wasting your time. I'm not saying anything until I render my decision."

"But, Mr. Mayor. This controversy has generated nationwide interest. It's almost as if you hold the deciding vote on the fate of Christmas. Can't you give the viewing audience some idea of just how you are going to vote."

"I'll make my statement to the full council. But it seems a little presumptuous to think that my decision here tonight will have much of an impact on Christmas anywhere but here in this town." G.D. turned went up the steps into the courthouse.

"Well, there you have it folks. The deciding vote is about to be cast. We will now switch to our cameras inside the council chambers and our correspondent Verna Dickerson. It's all yours, Verna."

"Thanks, Scoop." Verna said in a low voice. "We're here inside the council chambers where Mayor Steward is just making his way through the crowd to the front of the chambers. He's shaking hands with one or two, smiling and exchanging pleasantries. He just doesn't look like a man who might be holding the fate of Christmas in his hands."

G.D. took his seat at the table after greeting the other members of the council. There was a lot of conversation going on in the room. Some of it louder than others. G. D. hesitated for just a moment, then picked up his gavel and wrapped on the desk.

"Order. Order. Come on, folks. Settle down now. We need to get this meeting under way."

The crowd noise slowly subsided as every eye was turned toward him. G. D. took a deep breath.

"Thank you. The regularly scheduled meeting of the Newton's Mill City Council is called to order, and will be conducted according to established rules and procedures."

"Right, Mr. Mayor." J. B. Nickels spoke. "And that means first on the agenda is old business."

"And we all know what that means, don't we Mr. Mayor?" A voice called from the crowd. That started the talking again.

"Order." G. D. banged his gavel again and then sat quietly waiting for the noise to subside. When it had settled down he stood and surveyed the room. He saw people he had known most of his life. And lots of new faces that had moved to Newton's Mill in the last few years of steady growth. *"Well, here goes."* he thought.

****

Hebert arrived at the City Council chambers before most of the crowd. He took his seat at the usual spot and busied himself with looking over the agenda for the night's meeting. *"Looks like old business is first on the list."* He thought. *"Well, it will be good to get that over with."*

"Hello, Councilman Humble."

Hebert looked up to see Gabriel standing in front of the table. "Oh, hey, Gabriel. You're here early."

"Yes, thought I might have a chance to talk with you before everyone else got here."

"Sure," Hebert said, as he leaned back in his chair. "What's up?"

"I know things seem to be going wrong in your life right now."

"That's putting it mildly." Hebert smiled.

"Well, I just wanted to encourage you and tell you that everything is going to be fine. You'll get past this trouble, and your future will be full of all the happiness you have missed these many years."

"Thank you, Gabriel. But I have to ask you. You seem to know an awful lot about an awful lot of things. How is that so?"

"I'm just nosy, I guess." Gabriel said with a laugh.

"I don't think that's it all. When you're around I feel a peace, and...and..."

"Yes?"

"I guess I'll just come right out and say it. Love. At first I didn't recognize the feeling. It had been so long since I felt it. But, you just seem to exude a feeling of love."

"Love is a pretty strong emotion, Hebert."

"I know. I know. But the love I feel when you're around seems not to come exactly from you. I don't know just how to explain it. It's like an...an aura. No that's not the word I want. It's like the love is coming through you, from someplace else. Oh, I guess that sounds a little dumb, doesn't it?"

"Not really. In fact, you have pretty much got the picture. The love you feel is coming from somewhere else. I'm just the messenger, bringing a gift. I'm here because you needed to feel that love, especially with all that's going on right now in your life."

"But, where is it coming..." Hebert stopped in mid sentence. He suddenly knew just where it was coming from. A small tear formed at the corner of his eye. "I know." He said, softly. "Now I know. Thank you, Gabriel. It is a most wonderful gift."

"Yes, love is a most wonderful gift." Gabriel turned and walked away.

****

Ira Freethinker wasn't out in front picketing. In fact, he was sitting alone in the council chambers, waiting for the meeting to start. He hoped no one would notice him, or remember that he had made a fool of himself at the last meeting. He didn't want to be identified with the AAA anymore and so he tried to seem as inconspicuous as possible. It didn't work.

"Say, aren't you that Ira Freethinker guy? The one from the AAA?" It was Spike Morgan. He seemed to enjoy asking people tough questions. "What are you doing here?"

"Actually my name is John. John Smart. And I'm not with that group anymore."

"Well, if you ask me that's pretty smart, Mr. Smart. 'Cause you weren't makin' any friends in here the other night. It's a wonder old Reverend Brown didn't blitz you like he almost did that other guy."

"Who you callin' old, Spike?" Reverend Brown had come up behind them just in time to hear the boys comment."

"Oops. Sorry Reverend. Didn't mean anything by it. I'll see ya later." The boy got up and hurried away.

"So, Ira Freethinker. We meet again."

"No, Reverend Brown. Its just John, now. John Smart. I'm no longer a part of that group."

"Really? What made you change your mind?"

"A fellow named Gabriel."

"Ah, yes. Gabriel. I can see how he might do that. Tell me about it."

John filled the Reverend in on all that had happened the past week and how Gabriel had had such an impact on his life. And it seemed that the longer he talked about it the better he felt.

"You know Reverend, just talking with you about it makes me feel better. I was really feeling pretty lost."

"Sometimes confession is good for the soul, as my good friend Monsignor O'Rourke would say. I'm glad that Gabriel had such an impact on you. He's been pretty important in my life the last few days, too."

"I guess I owe you an apology for last Tuesday night. Now that I think back on it you would have probably been right if you had blitzed me, as the boy said."

"Well, I'm afraid my blitzing days are over. But I accept your apology and I'd like to invite you to church on Sunday." Reverend Brown shook John's hand. "There are some good people there who might like to call you a friend."

"Thank you, Reverend. I just might do that. It's been a while since I've had any friends."

"Good, now I've got to get around and see a few more people before the meeting starts. Good to meet you, John. I don't think I'm going to miss Ira at all."

" You know, I don't think I will, either."

J.B. and Cora came into the council chambers together. They spent some time talking to a few friends there and J.B. was just about to take his seat at the table when Gabriel walked up.

"Hello Mr. and Mrs. Nickels. How are you?"

"Gabriel." Cora said. "I was hoping you would be here tonight."

"Oh, I wouldn't miss this for the world. I think it's going to be a very interesting evening."

"To say the least." J.B. added. "I can't remember when there was so much interest in this little town. We seem to have become quite famous. Or infamous, depending on which side of the situation you're on."

"Well, I'm pretty much on the side of the Nativity Scene." Gabriel said. "But it will be interesting to see which way Mayor Steward votes."

"He's been pretty closed mouth about it." J.B. added. "So it could go either way. Well, I have to get in my seat before the proceedings get underway. Nice to see you again, Gabriel."

"You, too, Mr. Nickels." Gabriel said as J.B. walked away.

"I see what you mean about the change in him."

"It's wonderful, you know. He's so much calmer now. And everything isn't about the bottom line. Do you know he has had me set up two scholarship funds and we will be working with the charities here in Newton's Mill to fund some of their work? It's a miracle, Gabriel. A miracle."

"Mrs. Nickels, the man you're seeing now was always inside. It just needed to break out. The really important thing is that you stuck by him when he was so profit oriented and difficult to work with. Now you and he can begin to make a real impact on this town. That's the miracle."

"And I owe it all to you."

"No ma'am. I was just the messenger."

"The messenger?"

"Well, that is what Gabriel means." He said with a smile as he turned to leave. "The messenger."

****

"Good Evening, Hebert." Mary Beth Johnson said, as she took her seat next to him. Big night tonight, huh?"

"Hello, Mary Beth. Yes. Very big. Maybe the biggest night this little town has ever seen. Did you see all the reporters and TV cameras out side?"

"I sure did. And I see there's just about that many along the back wall in here. Did you talk to any of the reporters?"

"No, I sort of snuck in the back way and got to my seat before anyone could catch me. I don't feel much like talking to any reporters right now."

"Smart move. That Scoop fellow cornered me on my way in and wanted to know if I had any idea how G.D. was going to vote."

"What did you tell him?"

"I told him that even if I knew I wasn't about to tell him before it was announced at the meeting. Sometimes these TV types can be a real pain."

"True. But they have a tough job I guess. How are things down at the paper?"

"Rolling along, Hebert. Should be a big front page story after this meeting."

"Yeah, you should sell a ton of papers."

"Hebert, before this thing gets started I just wanted to tell you how sorry I was to hear about you and Bertha."

"News travels fast in this town." Hebert laughed. "But then, you are the editor of the newspaper, so I guess you would be up on the latest happenings."

"Well, this is one happening that won't be finding any space in my paper. But, just for your own information, I feel like this might be a good thing for you."

"Oh, it is, Mary Beth. It definitely is. And that is what makes it seem so unreal."

"Unreal?"

"Yes. You would think that a man whose wife just left him would be devastated."

"And you're not?"

"Mary Beth, do I look devastated to you?"

Mary Beth looked closely at Hebert for a few seconds, then smiled and shook her head. "No, Hebert, you sure don't look like a man that's devastated. In fact, you look like someone who has just had a great weight lifted from their shoulders."

"I am. I never quite realized just how Bertha had beaten me down until now. And it's my own fault. I let her run me like a railroad. Everything was for Bertha. But now, well, now I feel like that train has left the station and I'm on my way to a new life."

"I'll tell you, Hebert, most all of us, your friends, could see the changes taking place in you. But none of us had the courage to say anything to you about it."

"Probably wouldn't have done any good, anyway. It was just

easier to give in. But that's all behind me now. And I'm looking forward to a new life. It's going to be wonderful getting to know all my old friends again. It feels like I've been away a long time."

"Feels that way to us, too."

"Can I tell you something strange?"

"Off the record?"

"Off the record."

"Sure."

"Have you met that new fellow Gabriel?"

"Yes, he was in my office yesterday."

"Last Wednesday I ran into him in the parking lot at the Mall. He seemed to know me, even though I had never seen him before."

"Several people have had similar experiences, I believe."

"Anyway, we had a short conversation and then, as he left, he told me things were going to get better for me very soon. Do you suppose this is what he meant?"

"After hearing about his contact with others here in Newton's Mill it wouldn't surprise me a bit. Here's G.D. Looks like this is about to get underway."

****

"I know you all are waiting for my decision on the matter before us. But, before I give it, I think you should know how I arrived at that decision. It's been a very tough week for me. I was born in this town. And as I look around this room I see folks I have known all my life. As well as lots of new faces who have decided to make Newton's Mill their home."

There was complete silence in the room. G.D. noticed Gabriel standing off to one side at the back of the room. *"Is he smiling?"* He thought, just before continuing.

"This is a nice town. A town that folks can be proud to live in. It's also a town built on traditional values. Values like hard work, and paying your bills and being a good neighbor. It's a town where almost everyone attends one church or another and most of us try to live by the Good Book."

Reverend Brown and Monsignor O'Rourke nodded their heads in agreement, as did others in the crowd.

"Since I have been Mayor no other issue has ever had such an impact on Newton's Mill. Not even the water meter situation of a couple of years ago."

There were some chuckles and nodding heads among the audience. That had been a difficult period, as well.

"In fact, it would seem no other issue has had quite the impact on the state, or the country for that matter. Who would have thought that our town would be in the spotlight as it is? For most of the week I struggled to understand why this issue had taken on such importance. And then last night, it all became very clear to me. My decision here doesn't make any difference."

"What, what do you mean Mr. Mayor." Shouted someone from the back of the room. Others took up the question, as well.

"Order." G.D. banged his gavel, restoring order to the room. "To continue. Whether I vote in favor of, or against the Nativity Scene there will still be a celebration of Christmas. Putting the Nativity Scene on the Court House lawn, or not, won't keep Christmas from taking place in the hearts of men and women of peace. The Nativity Scene is a symbol. A symbol of a gift that was given to anyone who would receive it. Putting it on display just serves as a reminder of that gift.

Take a look at what we have done with Christmas. We have turned it into a commercial holiday, where the emphasis is on buying, and spending. Where the carols of the season are forbidden in our schools, where Season's Greetings, or Happy Holidays, has replaced the cheerful Merry Christmas. Where the tradition of gathering at the Nativity Scene on Christmas Eve has been replaced by last minute shopping, wrapping presents, and generally ignoring the true meaning of Christmas."

G.D. paused and looked around the room. All eyes were on him. There was no movement at all. It was as if everyone was frozen in time. And Gabriel's smile had grown larger.

"You can legislate, you can litigate, you can argue and you can demand, but you can't take Christ out of Christmas, no matter how you try. So, if you haven't figured it out by now, I cast my vote for the Nativity Scene, and for Peace on Earth, Good Will to Men, as the angels sang that night so long ago."

Just as he was about to continue he heard someone begin to applaud at the back of the room. He was shocked to see that it was Ira Freethinker, on his feet, then another person stood and joined him, followed by another, and another, until nearly the whole room was on it's feet. It took several minutes for order to be restored. When things were quiet again G.D. continued.

"Thank you. Thank you so much for that vote of confidence. Now, since there is no other business on the calendar for tonight, and before I close the meeting I would like to invite everyone to the Court House on Christmas Eve. That's one tradition that I think really needs to be revived. It's been too long."

G.D. banged his gavel. "Meeting adjourned." He said.

****

Christmas Eve

A light snow had begun to fall early in the afternoon and by six the ground was covered with a soft blanket of white. Newton's Mill had begun to slow down. The Mall, thanks to J.B. Nickels, had closed at noon, and wouldn't reopen until the day after Christmas. G.D. had given Jayne and the others the entire day off, as he did every Christmas, so that they could finish any last minute things they needed to do.

****

Hebert had put up a Christmas tree in his living room, in front of the big windows, for everyone to see. Bertha had never let him do that. She didn't want the mess. But he had bought the tree and lights, and tinsel and all the trimmings. He invited Katie, and Paul and Katie's Mom over to help him decorate and when they had finished they sat in front of the fireplace, drinking warm cider and admiring their handiwork.

****

John Smart, Richard Foster and Rufus Pettifogger had spent the days before Christmas volunteering with several of the charities in town and the three of them had become fast friends. They always seemed to be so joyful in everything they did. The three of them had finally found something they believed in.

****

Nate Archibald, much to his wife's relief, had given up any plans to run for any other office and was spending the days before Christmas calling friends and family and inviting them all to the Nativity Scene for Christmas Eve. He was much quieter and seemed to feel no urge to launch into long-winded speeches about mostly nothing at all. A fact greatly appreciated by all who knew him.

****

Bertha Humble spent the weeks before Christmas solidifying herself in the social scene of the big city and had no thoughts of Hebert, Newton's Mill, or Christmas, for that matter. She kept telling herself how happy she was. And, for awhile, she even believed it.

****

"Well, Helen," G.D. called from the front hall. "Are you about ready to go?"

"Just a minute, G.D. I'm just putting the finishing touches on. Have to look my best tonight. It's a special occasion."

"Hey, Dad. I'm ready." Gordon came into the hall, putting on his coat. "It's neat that it has started to snow, huh?"

"Yeah. Just wouldn't be Christmas without snow. But, no

snowballs tonight."

"Gee Dad, do you really think I would hit you with a snowball?" Gordon said, with a mischievous smile.

"Only if you got the chance." G.D. laughed.

"Well, here I am, boys." Helen said, as she came down the stairs.

G.D. and Gordon both whistled a long, slow whistle.

"Alright, you two. Enough of that. G.D. help me on with my coat."

"At your service, Madam." He said with a bow.

"Keep that up and I'll be the one to hit you with a snowball."

The three of them left the house and began the walk to the Court House. As they walked along they were joined by others headed in the same direction.

"Looks like there will be good turnout." G. D. thought.

****

Standing on the steps of the Court House were people from the choirs of several churches in the town. They had arrived a little early to warm up and now, as people began to gather in front of the building they started to sing. Soon they were joined by others in the group of watchers until everyone was singing. The sound of the music was picked up by the soft breeze and was carried to all parts of the town. Others, hearing the music, followed the sound and were soon a part of the growing group in front of the Nativity Scene. Artemis' wife, Samantha, had organized a group of ladies to pass out hot chocolate and hot cider to anyone who wanted it. And there were plenty of cookies to go around. Nearly everyone had at least one cup, and a cookie or two. The young ones had several, of both. There were smiles, and laughter, and cheery greetings of Merry Christmas, everywhere. And an old tradition was reborn.

****

Gabriel stood at a distance from the crowd. His time at Newton's Mill was almost over. He smiled as he watched the people gather, heard the carols being sung and the greetings being said.

"Yes, Lord." He said softly. "It does look like Newton's Mill hasn't forgotten Christmas. So, I guess I should be going."

He turned and started walking away. Then he stopped and turned back to look at the gathering one more time. "Oh, and Lord, thanks for the snow. It's a nice touch."

The End

Ray Newman and Bob Willey have been collaborating on various types of writing for more than twenty years. However, most of what they have done relates to their work as puppeteers. They have created dozens of scripts for presentations in Churches throughout the Northern California area.

Ray retired from the Army as a First Sergeant and has been writing for various mediums since his high school days. He is a member of the Quill and Scroll Big Inch Society and has had articles and stories published in several publications. He also writes verses for greeting card companies. He has taken a script originally prepared as a six night Children's Crusade and adapted it to a novel format. While Ray and Bob write together when preparing scripts, Ray adapts the scripts to novel format.

Bob is a retired teacher living in South Carolina and, like Ray, has been puppeteering for over twenty years. He presently heads the Puppet Ministry at his church and is constantly creating new avenues for presentation of the Gospel through puppetry.

Made in the USA
Columbia, SC
18 March 2019